The [...] ing Shelter shovel down the first food he had tasted in two days. The blouse she wore fell down over her olive colored shoulders and showed a great deal of promising cleavage.

Shell watched her closely and the more he ate, the more hungry he became—for her.

"I've got an idea or two," Shell said slyly.

But before he could finish, Conchita asked, "Why are you here? Are you here to kill people, to make trouble for Conchita?"

"No," Shell laughed. "I got separated from my people. I'm with the circus."

"You are no circus man, I can see that. There is more involved, I know this."

"You think so?" Shell sat down on Conchita's bed and he took off his hat. "Why do you think so?"

"Because I know La Condesa."

"La Condesa?"

"The countess—La Condesa Villa Real. The circus went to her ranch. And La Condesa cares nothing for fun and games, she cares only for wealth and power."

"There's business I have to attend to, and it looks like it'll have to be solved at the condesa's rancho."

"There is only one solution on that rancho, señor. All problems are solved by death— that is a place men go only to die . . . "

#6

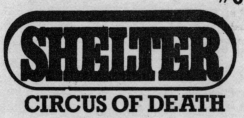

CIRCUS OF DEATH

BY
PAUL LEDD

ZEBRA BOOKS

KENSINGTON PUBLISHING CORP.

ZEBRA BOOKS

are published by

KENSINGTON PUBLISHING CORP.
21 East 40th Street
New York, N.Y. 10016

Printed in the United States of America

1.

The snow was heavy in the high passes and thunder echoed down the canyons, yet the cabin was warm and snug. The woman slipped from the bed and stoked the fire in the potbelly stove and the tall man, yawning sleepily in the cold gray light of dawn, watched her with interest as she moved about the room.

The fire sparked and the flames built to a warm glow. Wavering shadows danced across Nelly's lush naked body, her flesh highlighted and reddened by the firelight. She turned with a smile.

"You were sleeping; it was getting cold."

"I'm awake now," Shelter answered, and she crossed to the bed, her feet silent against the floor of the cabin, her full breasts swaying pendulously.

She slipped in beside him and her hair fell across his chest as she bent her lips to it, kissing him gently. She toyed with the dark hair on Shelter Morgan's hard-muscled torso, kissed him there again and then lifted her lips to his, pressing herself against him in a lingering, warming kiss.

Shelter kissed her in return, finding her mouth, her pulsing throat through the soft veil of her hair. Nelly lay on top of him, her eyes bright. Shelter let his hands run down her smooth back, across her soft buttocks, and he nuzzled her shoulders as she watched him tenderly.

Nelly rolled onto her side and Shelter followed, his hand running down her thigh and then up again, resting on the soft patch of hair between her warm thighs.

Nelly's head rolled back and Shell's lips went to her breasts, finding the pink nipples taut and eager, and he lingered lovingly over them as Nelly's encouraging hand stroked his hair, his back.

Outside the wind shrieked through the trees. The snow was falling heavily although they could not see it through the ice-glazed windows. Inside it was warm, with none of the wind finding a breach in the tightly chinked log walls.

There was only the dancing fire, the soft beating of the woman's heart. Shelter kissed Nelly's lips, feeling her hand slip across his abdomen, going to his crotch where she found his eager erection.

Gently she stroked him, searching him, inflaming Shelter's desire. His own hand lay nestled in her soft, curly bush like a bird sleeping in a quiet nest; now it awakened and his fingers roamed through it, finding the sensitive, already erect tab of flesh which lay hidden there, awaiting his touch.

Shelter's fingers flickered across it as Nelly's hand fondled his cock. Slowly her legs spread apart and Shelter let a finger dip inside of her warmth, finding her dewy, soft, ready for him.

Their mouths met in a hungry kiss as Shell rolled slightly toward Nelly, still touching her and then he felt Nelly position the head of his erection, rubbing it against the base of her clitoris as his finger dipped deeply inside of her.

Nelly's other hand joined them, and their fingers intertwined, stroked and fondled each other. Nelly still moved Shelter's cock against herself, and the sensitive touch of her warmth sent his pulse racing. Nelly's head lolled back against the pillow, her tongue touching her lips as she brought herself and Shell to a needful peak.

Then Shell could stand the waiting no longer, and neither could Nelly. He felt her guide the head of his shaft downward and hold it just at the warm entrance while Shelter shifted slightly, holding himself back.

Then he eased forward and Nelly's fingers drew him in inch by inch, her breathing shallow and quick as she felt him slip through her fingers and into her.

Nelly's hand moved across Shelter's thigh lovingly and then it went between his legs as she cradled his balls, holding them as he touched bottom with his cock.

Side by side they lay quietly, with Nelly's top leg thrown over Shelter's. Her mouth was open to Shelter's kiss, her tongue probing his mouth. Shelter could feel her quivering inside, her muscles working magic against his swollen erection.

Then Nelly began to sway against him, moving slowly, her pelvis grazing his as she let the slow sensations trickle through her body. But the drive was building in her and she could not slow it.

She clung to Shelter, kissing his throat, his shoulders, and her hips began to move in tight, demanding circles. Shelter rocked against her, and she drove her body against his, her hands tearing at him, clenching his hard buttocks, finding his shaft tearing at him, clenching his hard buttocks, finding his shaft again where he entered her. She stroked him there with her fingers as her whole body writhed in anticipation.

"I can feel it coming..." Nelly breathed into his ear. "Feel everything starting to come..." she touched her teeth to his ear, taking tiny bites. Her hips swayed as her voice dropped to a low, sensual moaning and she felt herself come undone, felt the swelling need which had been building burst in an explosive climax.

She was panting, her fingers travelling his body from his thighs to his neck, her lips kissing wherever they reached and Shelter felt his own climax building, felt the throbbing in his loins build as he began filling Nelly with long, deliberate strokes.

"Don't hold back, Shell. I want to feel it. Want to know I've made you feel good."

Her hands were gentle on his flesh now, running silkily across his buttocks and his thighs as he worked against her, his lips taking one nipple and then the other hungrily into his mouth as the rising tempo of his strokes led him to the brink of a quaking orgasm.

"Now..." Nelly whispered into his ear. "Oh ... I like that. I like you deep."

And then he came, deeply, and he lay against her, his body draining, Nelly's warmth enveloping him, her satisfied, nonsense whispering soothing, birdlike as her hands roamed his hard body, her heart still racing.

"Such a winter," Nelly breathed.

"It has been good." Shell ran a hand up along Nelly Dierks' arm, touching her lips with a finger.

"The two of us alone, snowed in. Of course when my brother and I first moved to Wyoming we were snowed in so bad we never left the cabin. *That* was the longest winter I ever spent!"

"And this one?"

"The shortest. Far too short, Shelter . . . unless you've changed your mind."

"You know I haven't, I can't."

"Well then . . . " She tried to laugh but a trace of disappointment was evident. She held him tightly one last moment before rising abruptly from the bed. "I'll get some breakfast."

It was still warm and so Nelly only slipped on an apron, going to the stove to make coffee and toast. They hadn't seen an egg the winter long, and most of the venison was gone, but Shelter didn't have his usual appetite anyway, and what they had was plenty.

After breakfast he would have to get dressed and stamp through the snow to feed the stock. The hay was getting short, but it looked like the snows were letting up and Nelly would have enough to last her through the spring.

Sliding sleepily to the edge of the bed, Shelter put his feet to the floor and scratched his head. Nelly was at the stove, making a deal more ruckus than she needed to—she had a touch of the pique today.

Parting was never easy. Nelly had known it was coming, but it had seemed a long time off last fall when they had patched up the burned out cabin and settled in for a long, loving winter. Now it was right on top of her and she was having some difficulty facing up to it.

Shell crossed to the mirror on the wall and dipped into the basin, splashing water on his face. Then he shaved, still naked, and Nelly who had turned to place the coffee sack back into the pantry stopped and watched, her eyes sweeping over the tall, hard body of Shelter Morgan.

In the mirror she could see his hard-edged face, those cool blue-gray eyes which she knew were capable of much laughter. Her eyes lingered another minute on Shelter as he scraped the dark stubble from his jaw, and she tried to take him all in.

His shoulders were broad, his back rippled as he moved. His waist was as narrow as Nelly's own. His thighs were heavily muscled, tapering. He was all man, that one . . . she turned away quickly and put the coffee away with a bang.

Shelter's eyes lifted to hers from the mirror and without saying a word Nelly went back to her breakfast making.

Shell finished up and brushed back his dark hair a little. Then, still undressed, he crossed to the table and sat down, hunkering over a cup of coffee as he watched Nelly who was worth the watching.

Wearing only that apron, she was turning the toast over the fire, her smooth white ass poking invitingly out. It was a delight for the eyes and Shell felt himself stirring again. He smiled.

11

"You mad at me, Nell?"

"Mad? A little—but you're a hell of a man to try stayin' mad at, Shelter Morgan. I'm mad *for* you," she said thoughtfully. "You be careful you don't spill that coffee!" she said more loudly than she intended. "It's hot —and we don't want to lose anything."

She placed a stack of toast on a plate before Shelter and watched as he ate, chasing it down with the strong, dark coffee.

Nelly's hands were folded before her, her chin resting on them. "I just don't want you to go—and I know you're going," she said finally.

"Yes, I am," Shelter answered quietly. "I've things to do."

"Like getting yourself killed! My God, Shelter, you've been shot, throwed, stabbed and beaten . . . you'd think a man would get the idea through his hard head that sooner or later some of that is going to stick!"

"It would seem so," Shelter answered with a grin. "I guess I got a head that's somewhat harder than usual."

"That's not all," Nelly said shyly. Then her serious vein returned and she watched the tall man eat. "I just don't understand, that's all. Most folks would be happy enough to walk wide of trouble. You, you're chasing it. We could have a fine life here in these mountains—have it any way you wanted it. I'd never push at you."

"I know it." Shell looked up and now those

12

eyes were hard, sparking and Nelly involuntarily flinched. "There's still ghosts riding with me, Nell. I still owe some men for what they did. There's some cold murderers out there living free and handsome while my boys lie dead in their graves."

"The law..." Nelly began, but Shelter cut her off.

"We've been through all that—you know the story. And," he reminded her, "you above all others should know that there is no law in this part of the country, that what there is is widely scattered, and a good half of them are either crooked or simply trying to make an easy living."

"I haven't forgotten about Wilson Clark," Nelly said, "how it was before you showed up."

"I didn't think you had."

"But after all this time... I would think your anger would have faded, that your need to find these men would have settled."

"It should have, maybe. Maybe one day it will. But no," Shelter shook his head, "I still see Dinkum, Thornton in my sleep, see the ambush guns opening up on us, see the men who were supposed to be our comrades, our officers behind their gunsights."

"With the war so nearly over, it must have sickened you to see your men die like that—killed by their own."

"It sickened me, Nelly. It's a sickness I still have to deal with. After all, I was respon-

13

sible. I was in charge, maybe I shoud have seen through that plot which General Custis, Colonel Fainer and the others had hatched."

"You were a good soldier, that's all. When they told you about the gold that had been left behind the Union lines, they impressed upon you how much that gold could do for your men. The medical supplies, the food, the clothing! You did what you had to, Shelter. You couldn't know they wanted the gold themselves; that they wanted to make the war pay."

"I wonder," Shell said, "just how many men they did kill by stealing that gold. The pain they caused, the suffering. God, Nell, there were boys layin' in the snow with an arm shot away, a leg crushed with no blanket to warm them, with no food to fill their shrunken bellies, with no morphine to drive out the horrible pain . . . that's what those twenty greedy, murderous men did. I can't forget it. I can't turn my back on it . . . ever."

Nell nodded and got up from the table, knowing she had pushed Shelter into talking about it more than he wanted. When he recalled it the pain showed in his eyes and it was intense enough for Nell to feel.

She wondered how it had felt at the bloody moment. Returning from that suicidal mission across the lines, successful when he had no right to be, then to have that feeling of triumph shattered. To be surrounded suddenly by his own men, his own officers and to watch the guns open up, spewing death. She knew he dreamed of it at times and awoke in a sweat.

She vowed then and there that she would not mention it again, not try to talk him out of his vengeance. If he loved her enough he would be back one day; if he did not, then it would never last anyway.

Shelter Morgan had been good to her. He had fought for her. Loved her. Built up this burned out cabin. She had asked for enough and had gotten it; she would ask for no more.

"Any chance of a little more toast, Nelly?" Shelter asked.

"Sure."

She sliced off two more slabs of bread from the loaf and held them over the fire. Glancing around she saw Shelter watching her. He had an elbow on the table, his chin in his hand and his eyes were on her buttocks which protruded from the apron back.

"Sure do like that," Shelter said, catching Nell's eyes on him.

"I know you do," she said, her eyes bright. "But you can't mean you're ready again? We just . . ."

"I just had a plate full of toast, too, Nell. But I believe I would like just a little more to get me through the morning."

"You're a rascal," Nell laughed. Soberly she added, "And a hell of a man, I don't know what I'll do when you're gone."

Shelter stood, pushing back his chair and

he walked around the table, a naked savage thing. Nell felt her heart skip a beat as her eyes fell to his growing erection.

"God, you're a stud," she breathed.

Shelter was to her now and he pulled Nell into his arms, kissing her searchingly. She answered his kiss, putting her arms around his neck, hanging on as her emotions turned her legs to jelly.

"I do like that apron," Shell said. He kissed her ear and nuzzled her throat. "I truly do like that get-up, Nelly." Then without another word, he turned her away from him, facing her toward the table.

Nelly leaned forward, putting her hands on the table top and Shelter parted the curtains at the back of that apron, leaing forward to plant a kiss on her smooth white buttocks.

Then he slipped up behind her, lifting and spreading her as he came nearer. Nelly was bent far forward now and by looking between her legs she could watch as Shelter slid the head of his cock between the soft folds of her flesh and she trembled with anticipation, watching as the shaft slipped between her legs and filled her with a new warmth.

Nelly bowed her head to the table, still watching with fascination as Shelter began to thrust against her. He liked it that way, and he could feel his need growing quickly as his hands clutched at Nelly's ass. Then he lifted her higher and stroked deeply, her warmth surrounding him, her juices beginning to flow.

Nelly's arms were folded on the table. Her face was hidden beneath a profusion of hair. Now she began to move in concert, sliding backward and forward feeling his pelvis slamming against her as his pace quickened and she knew that Shelter would come quickly.

His rough hands kneaded her buttocks, his cock filled her to the limit, bringing every nerve ending inside of Nelly to flashing life. The light blinked on in her head and she moved savagely against Shelter, wanting to find her peak as rapidly as he did.

There was a need in Shelter, a terrible hunger for Nelly just then. He wanted to buck against her, to fill her, to know that she was coming with him. And he worked against her roughly, hearing the tiny, distant gasps from her lips, feeling her trickle her warmth against him.

Then, abruptly Nelly lifted her head and she went tense, the cords of her neck taut, her hips shaking convulsively as she found her climax, as Shelter filled her with his own quaking orgasm.

"God . . . " Nelly puffed. She let her head rest again on the table, her breath coming raggedly. "I've got to wear this apron more," she gasped.

They made their way to the bed where they lay quietly for most of an hour, their breathing slowing as they exchanged tender kisses, tiny touches. Outside the wind still shrieked, but through the window they could see bright sunlight.

"Looks like the storm's letting up," Shelter said.

"It could be all over."

"Could be."

Then Shelter kissed Nelly's shoulder and wiped the hair from her face. He sat up and swung to the side of the bed. "I'll see to the stock while there's a break in the weather."

Nelly did not answer, but she attempted a smile which came out weakly. She watched as Shell dressed and slipped into his sheepskin.

The sunlight was bright through the door as he opened it and Nelly felt the cold draft. Then he was gone and she lay her head down on her pillow, watching the ceiling for a long while.

There was two feet of new snow in the yard as Shelter Morgan stepped out. The wind was playing Katie-bar-the-door in the pines and the pines swayed before it. The far mountains stood aloof and white against a somber sky. The earth was brilliant white and deep shadow; the pine forest spread off toward eternity beyond the ranch.

Shelter tramped through the snow and went into the barn, picking up a pitchfork. The black gelding he had adopted lifted its head and nickered with recognition and Shelter went to it, stroking the horse's neck.

He gave the black an extra portion of oats from the dwindling supply in the bin. It would be a long ride to Kansas City.

18

Shelter gave the horse a slap on the rump and pitched some hay to Nelly's horses and the milk cow which lowed miserably, rolling brown eyes at Shell.

He cleaned up a little then and walked back to the barn door, watching the clouds shift across the far-reaching sky. The pine scent was heavy in the air, the stable smells. Water dripped from the barn roof and fell to the ground at Shell's feet, pocking the snow as the sun melted the icicles.

It was over. Winter, Wyoming, that little dark-eyed girl in the house, would all be in the past soon. He leaned on the pitchfork handle and looked it all over, imprinting it on his memory.

There would be no coming back, he knew already.

And he wondered what kind of man he truly was to leave it all and return to the lonesome trails, the hard times, the killing.

He walked back to the house then and sat to the table, oiling his guns as Nelly watched silently.

2.

Shelter trailed out in the early morning light. The dawning flushed the snow-swept peaks to a rose color and etched deep shadows before the pines. The smoke from the cabin rose lazily into the crystal of the sky, but now the cabin was sinking behind the ranks of spruce, and all but the chimney was lost to sight.

Shelter knew she was still standing there, arms folded, watching after him; but he did

20

not look back. The cabin had already become a thing of the past, Nelly's love a distant if warm memory. He rode on across the timbered slopes, thinking not of the comforts that lay behind but of the long road ahead.

The snow around the Green River trading post was drifted high, but Willie Cashion was on the porch waiting when Shelter rode in. Shell swung down and took Willie's hand warmly. They had been through a fight together — that is a bond that draws men close in a relatively short time.

"Good to see you, partner," the lean cowboy said. "Thought maybe you wouldn't be comin' down at all." Willie's eyes lifted to the far mountains? "How's Nell?"

"She's fine. Just fine."

"Good." Willie draped an arm over Shell's shoulder and they walked inside. "I take it that Shadow Box got through with my note. I wondered about that — the snow was deep."

"He got through. Those Shoshoni can walk through a blizzard fifty miles and not miss the mark by ten feet."

"He's good all right." Willie sat to the table and called for some coffee. "He remembered you — and your silver dollars," Willie said with a grin. "That hard money's tough to come by for a Shoshoni."

"I gave him a few dollars," Shell said, "and an extra blanket — I'm not sure which he appreciated more."

The wall behind Willie Cashion was planked, hung with bits of harness and new bridles. Across the way was the general store itself, with bales of new jeans, sacks of flour, sugar and salt, new rifles and shelves of tinned goods.

Charlie Staggs who owned the trading post wandered over and slapped down a coffeepot between them. He nodded to Shelter, "Out of hibernation?"

"Finally made it down," Shell answered.

After Charlie had walked back to the counter to take care of two fur-clad mountain men, Shelter lifted his eyes to Willie. "Well, what can you tell me?"

"All I know was in that letter, Shell," Willie replied with a shrug. "It was in Kansas City that Rafer ran into him—you remember Rafer."

"Very well," Shell answered.

"Well he made that long cattle drive down there with the Circle Deuce. So Rafe is resting up, having his fling—makin' sure he don't come back with no money—God, that'll ruin a cowboy—and he sees the name, Roland Blue. That's the name, ain't it. Roland Blue?"

"It is," Shelter answered. "Seargeant Roland Y. Blue. He was one of them that ambushed us back there in Georgia."

"That's what I recollected. Rafer, he should know—he's carryin' that list you copied out for him like a lot of the boys are now."

Shell nodded. That thought had come to him and he had been distributing the list to the men

22

he knew and trusted in Wyoming. Men he had fought with in the range wars. These cowboys were a travellin' lot, and sooner or later they were bound to cross someone's trail. It looked like Rafer had.

Shelter recalled Blue well. A burly, redheaded NCO out of Alabama, he had been slovenly, surly, drunken. The last time Shell had seen him, down along the Conasauga River, Blue was squeezing the trigger on a revolver which was aimed at Shell's head.

"How did Rafer happen to spot Blue's name?" Shell asked. "It doesn't seem a man with his background would be splashing it around."

"Hell, the way Rafer tells it he couldn't miss that name, Shelter. It was painted all over the side of a circus tent."

"A circus?"

"That's what Rafer says." Willie finished his coffee and stood, watching the tall man with the cool blue eyes. "You think it's some kind of mistake? Someone with the same name or something?"

"Could be," Shell admitted. "Roland Blue — is that a common name, Willie?"

"Not much. The thing is, Shelter, Kansas City . . . ? That's a hell of a long ride to check this out."

"I've got to do it, Willie. If it is Blue, I won't let him get away, and Rafer seemed sure." Shell shook his head and stood, taking Willie's hand. "I'll be ridin', pal. I guess I won't be back this way again."

"Well, luck to you then Shell. Thanks for all you done for us."

"You did your own share, Willie." Shelter tugged on his hat and walked to the door. Together they watched the bright sunshine on the new snow, watched the wisps of clouds drift past the high, cold mountains.

"Watch out for those bad steers, Willie." Shelter swung into the saddle and sat there for a minute, just gazing at the pine clad mountains beyond the trading post.

"Shelter . . . " Willie was hesitant.

"What is it, Will?"

"You're riding. Like you say, you probably won't be back." The cowboy scratched his arm and looked at the ground.

"And?"

"It's Nell. I always took kind of a shine to her. Would you mind . . . if I kinda looked her up?" Willie smiled sheepishly and Shell shook his head.

"I think it'd be great for both of you, Willie. You know she still could really use a man on that place. Outside of patching the cabin I didn't have time to do much. She'd like it, I think. Someone around."

"You think so?" Willie's expression brightened.

"I expect so, Will."

"Maybe then . . . one of these days soon. I just might ride on by her place."

"Don't wait too long, Willie. There'll be another man. She's a hell of a woman."

24

Then Shelter tugged his hat lower against the glare of the sun and turned that big black gelding, riding through the snow of the trading post yard, heading south as Willie Cashion watched, lifting a hand in farewell.

The day was clear and cold, the sun brilliant as Shelter rode southward. The Green River, swollen with snowmelt flowed past, carrying uprooted trees.

A *circus.* Now what was there to be made of that? Blue a circus man? It was nearly incredible. Yet as Willie said, it could be a mistake. Mistake or not, though, Shelter was going through to KC.

It was a long trip, a long ride, but Shell had no intention of riding much of the way. The train ran through Fort Bridger which was fifty miles south by west. From there it should be possible to ride the rails most of the way to Kansas City, with maybe a gap in the connecting lines here and there. There were stories that the Cheyenne had torn up some track east of Laramie.

But inside of a week, at the outside, Shelter expected to hit Kansas City. It was crazy in a way, Shell supposed, but he had ridden longer trails tracking these butchers. It could very well be that Rafer was mistaken. But if he wasn't, Shell wanted to find out first hand.

Even saying it was actually Roland Blue whom Rafer had run into, that had been quite a time back. Those circus people had a habit of not staying in one place for long.

But Shelter had made his mind up, and he was moving. The cold air felt good, the easy gait of a good horse beneath him was familiar, pleasurable. Shell had never been one for sitting, planning, waiting.

Now that part of it was over and he was on the move, with a definite goal no matter how distant. Fording the Green a mile upstream from Bridger he looked back once toward the high mountains of Wyoming, and with a smile he thought again of Nelly Dierks and of Willie. It would be the last time for a long while—his thoughts were on Kansas City now, on the butcher named Roland Blue.

Kansas City was booming when Shelter hit town six days after leaving Fort Bridger. Ellsworth and Dodge City were already slowly dying towns and KC, taking up the slack, had become a thriving railhead, its cattle pens bursting at the seams with Texas beef.

The streets were dusty, dry and the boardwalks—and especially the saloons—were crowded with cowboys washing the dryness out of their throats. Shell counted sixteen saloons in a row up Cable Street. Each of them seemed to be booming.

The wind was light, off the Missouri River, and it cooled the sweat which trickled down Shelter's throat. From across town the cattle smells drifted.

If the hotel had a name it wasn't posted, but they had a room. Shelter signed in and then waited impatiently for the clerk who finally arrived from a back room, rubbing his eyes sleepily.

He glanced at the signature and yawned.

"Two bucks."

Shelter slid him two silver dollars and the clerk grabbed a brass key from behind the counter.

"Sixteen. Upstairs to the end," he told Shell.

"Is there a bath to be had?"

"You'll have to try the barber shop. We gave up on baths. Wasn't no call for 'em, besides, when the water splashes over upstairs the roof leaks down below."

"I'll try the barber shop," Shell answered without a smile. "And I'm lookin' for some entertainment."

The clerk learned far across the counter and said from the side of his mouth. "There's a girl . . . "

"I heard there was a circus in town," Shell interrupted.

"That's long gone," the clerk answered, waving a hand, "but if you want some *real* entertainment . . . "

"Not just now," Shell replied. He shouldered his saddlebags then and took his Winchester from the counter, turning to stride up the stairs. The desk clerk watched after him a minute, shrugging. Then he went to sorting the mail.

"What was that, Ollie?" a voice behind him inquired.

"Oh, it's you, Mister Luther. What was what?"

"That conversation with the cowboy." He glanced at the register, reading the signature.

"Nothin'. He asked for a bath . . . oh, and he asked if that circus wasn't still in town."

"The circus." Luther lifted his hooded eyes to the stairwell and touched his thin mustache thoughtfully. Then he nodded to himself and strode away. The desk clerk watched as Luther, dressed impeccably in a pearl gray suit and white planter's hat, walked to the front door and went out into the sunlight.

Ollie's forehead furrowed up and he pondered it for a moment. Making nothing out of it, he shrugged again and returned to sorting the mail.

Tandy Luther stood for a moment on the boardwalk in front of the hotel, watching a pair of cowboys ride slowly past, their eyes measuring the saloons. From uptown a train whistle blew.

Luther noticed the big black gelding tied to the rail, its cinches loose, its head low. Obviously it had been ridden a way. He walked to it, glancing back toward the hotel door. Circling the horse he noticed the HW brand, but it meant nothing to him. Whoever the tall man was, he was no local cowboy, nor was he attached to any of the major Texas crews —Luther knew the book on those brands.

Shoving his hands into his pockets, Tandy Luther stepped back onto the boardwalk, standing for a moment in the narrow ribbon of shade next to the building.

Whoever the tall man was, he had come a long way. A long way to trouble. Of course, he considered, it could be nothing. Only a bored saddle tramp inquiring about a circus, but Luther didn't believe it.

He had seen fighting men before, plenty of them, and this man had the cut about him. He wore that gun like he knew how to use it. Well, Luther thought grimly, he would have every opportunity. He turned on his heel and strode across the dusty street toward the telegraph office.

Shelter opened the door to his room, checked the springs on the sagging bed and opened the window, letting a blast of fresh, dry air into the musty room. Then he placed his saddlebags over the back of the chair and rinsed off in the wash basin, studying his sunburned, stubble-darkened face in the gray mirror.

His body was gritty, sticky. He would have that bath. First the horse must be seen to and then he would walk to the barber shop for a hot tub. After that he would find him one of those Kansas City steaks and see if they lived up to their reputation.

Then the serious work must begin.

It was still incredible that Blue could be somehow attached to a circus, but apparently he was. The circus was long gone, the desk clerk assured him. Fine—but a circus does not travel secretly, nor does it travel quickly.

Someone would have seen it roll out, and Shelter would follow. And if Blue was there to be found, Shelter would find him.

It was cooling, afternoon settling to dusk as Shelter left the stable where he had put up the black, taking the time to rub it down and curry it himself. Uptown a few lights spotted the twilight. The saloon hitch rails were lined with ponies shoulder to shoulder; it looked like a big drive had just rolled in.

The barber shop was empty but for a single customer—a town man with muttonchop whiskers and a look of affluence about him.

The barber, a tall narrow man with a curled mustache, glanced up as Shelter strode through the door, causing a tiny attached bell to tinkle.

"I'll be with you in a minute," he told Shelter.

"I can wait. I'll be wanting a bath too."

"Joey!" The barber called back over his shoulder. A kid of eight or nine, a replica of the barber minus the mustache, appeared from the back. "This man needs a bath."

The barber frowned in concentration, wiped a bit of lather from the town man's chin with his thumb and took a careful, practiced stroke with his razor.

"Go with the kid," he told Shell.

Shelter strode to the back room where three wooden tubs side by side lined a wall. He stripped down while the kid went off some-where to get hot water.

Shelter started to step into the tub when the kid reappeared. "Best wait a minute," the boy said, "this water'll boil you."

It was hot. Steam rolled up into the air as the kid emptied the five gallon pot and returned for another.

"Dad's havin' pipes put in next year. We got us a big boiler out back." He sighed wearily. "I won't miss the totin'."

Shelter settled into the tub, his skin object-ing to the temperature. Once in, however, the water soothed him, soaking into tired muscles, saddle sore joints.

The kid brought a scrub brush, a wash rag and a bar of lye soap strong enough to lift the grime without scrubbing. Then the kid perched on a barrel, watching as Shelter washed.

"That a bullet hole in your chest?" he in-quired. Shelter nodded.

"I got that from not mindin' my own business. Say," he asked the boy, "I heard there was a circus in town."

The kid's eyes lighted up. "There sure was. It was a dandy. I went twice. I woulda gone back but pa wouldn't let me."

"A good one, was it?" Shell scrubbed his toes and glanced at the boy.

"I should smile! They had tigers, a bear and paradin' pachyderms—that's what the man called 'em," he added sheepishly. "Ele-phants."

31

"Sounds like some show."

"It was. They had these folks that could fly through the air." He glanced around at the outer door, "And a woman with 'em, wearin' nothin' but red underwear. A man with tattoos on his whole entire body . . . a sword swallower . . . "

"But it's gone now?" Shell interrupted.

"All folded up and gone two weeks back. You missed out, I'm afraid."

"I don't know." Shell stepped from the tub, accepting a towel. "I'm a travellin' man. Maybe I'll catch up with them down the trail. Where was it they were headed?"

"South. New Orleans, I heard a man say. They rolled them wagons up onto a sternwheeler and was gone on down that Missouri with their brass band playin'."

Shelter buttoned up his shirt and tucked it in, tossing the kid a quarter. New Orleans, was it? Well he had never seen it, and maybe it was time. He had hoped to run the circus down quickly, but if they had taken a steamboat downriver, they were making better time than Shelter could on horseback.

The barber was ready for him when he stepped into the shop and he settled into the chair as the man whipped a sheet across him, stropping the razor to a fine edge.

"Where's the steamboat office?" Shelter asked.

"Front Street. Six blocks east." Then the barber lifted Shell's nose and began whisking off that beard stubble. Shelter let him trim his hair which was hanging nearly to his shoulders now and then he had some bay rum slapped on.

When he stepped from that chair he felt like a new man. The barber brushed him off and he pulled his hat on, examining himself in the mirror. His cheeks were lighter beneath the whiskers and a fine white scar still showed across his jaw from away back in Arizona.

"That all right?" the barber asked.

"Fine." He gave the man two dollars and stepped out onto the boardwalk. It was growing dark fast now, a last red cloud floating low in the western sky. Uptown a piano was playing and the streets were growing crowded.

Shelter walked back to the hotel and went up to his room, smelling beef roasting somewhere below. He swung open the door and stopped, puzzled.

Something was not right, but he couldn't put his finger on it. He tossed his hat on the bed and went to his saddlebags, wanting the fresh shirt he had stowed in them. That indefinable something still bothered him, nudging his mind.

And then it got another nudge. Someone had been in his saddlebags. A man packs a certain way on the trail, wanting the articles he uses most on the top in easy reach. After many trails, enough time on the move habit takes over and items are positioned just so—unless someone else has been into the kit.

Someone had. Shell sat down on the bed and glanced around. He was certain of it. He pulled the shirt from the saddlebags and went to the mirror, buttoning it up.

It was then, as he reached the top button, that it hit him. He knew just what that indefinable something had been, because it was stronger on his fresh shirt.

It was lavender powder, a woman's powder. Whoever it had been, it was a she-woman. The window had been left wide open and the breeze off the Missouri River was fresh, cold, but it couldn't erase that scent.

Shell turned and walked to the window. The streets were busy, the saloons lit up. Kansas City was alive with cowboys, river men, buyers and emigrants.

And at least one woman who wore lavender powder and liked going through men's bags.

It bothered Shelter because nothing had been taken, nothing disturbed. Of course there was really nothing there *to* take; but someone rifling luggage for valuables wouldn't have been so careful.

That meant that the woman, whoever she was, was not interested in money, but in Shelter Morgan himself.

3.

Shelter's cabin was on the port side, astern. But just now he was at the rail, watching the sun sparkle on the slow running Missouri as the sternwheel paddled against the water, pushing the *Alabama Maid* downstream past the isolated farms, the small towns along the banks.

Now and then they passed a slower moving keel boat, usually laden with furs from the northern mountains, and twice they had passed big white steamers laboring upcurrent carrying supplies to Saint Joe or Kansas City. Along the decks of these paddle wheelers Shelter could make out young hopeful faces. Greeners, sodbusters, folks heading west looking for living space and a new life.

They had traveled the easy portion of their journey. Now it would begin—the cholera, the dust storms, the raiding Indians, the ground so hard it could not be plowed. Drought, hailstorms, marauding locusts and hard winters out on the plains where no trees grew, where nothing cut the wind, where the women were killed by loneliness just as frequently as their men were killed by the hard labor.

But they would endure. They would build a land out there because they wanted it. Wanted it more than anything else.

"Pleasant sight, isn't it?"

Shelter turned to glance at the tall man in white beside him at the rail. He was mate on the vessel, a man named Trumpy who had nearly white hair and mustaches despite being in his twenties.

"It is. Must be a fair life steaming up and down."

"It's soft. Pretty. Funny thing, not many of us stay on board for long. A sailor, any sailor, is a rambling man. I signed on to get away from the wild oceans, high seas and hurricanes. Now . . . I'll be damned if I don't miss that sailing life. How's your trip been?" he asked Shell.

36

"Real comfortable. You know, I was wondering. My partner came down a while back and he said the damned boat smelled of elephant."

Trumpy laughed out loud. "That was the Marci K. They had a circus on board. They're still trying to scrub that smell out. Say, Morgan, we're getting up a faro game tonight in the dining room—how about a little low-stakes?"

"Not for me. The stakes couldn't be low enough just now."

"Well, drop on around anyway," Trumpy said. "The wine is free and there'll be conversation."

Trumpy slapped Shelter on the shoulder and went forward along the deck, chuckling to himself over the plight of the Marci K.

Shelter yawned and walked slowly around the deck, watching as the pilot guided the *Alabama Maid* to midstream to avoid a sandbar and a nearly hidden sawyer. He was nearly ready to return to his cabin when he saw her.

Tall, with slashing dark eyes and fine dark hair which glistened in the sunlight, she turned a haughty glance upon Shelter Morgan.

She seemed the lady, elegant and aloof. And she did not smile as Shelter appreciatively studied her figure, those delightfully upthrust breasts which showed as soft promises above the satin fabric of her dress.

She watched him woodenly, her eyes sharp, but when Shell gave her a wink her eyes brightened with laughter and her generous mouth turned down in a suppressed smile. Shell touched his hat brim and walked past, stopping once to look back at her. And when he did he found the woman still watching him. He grinned then and she turned her head away.

Whistling, Shelter walked to his cabin, watching the dark, willow clotted shoreline where the sun had already begun to fade.

Trumpy was standing outside the wheelhouse, nervously puffing on his pipe for a full half an hour before the second man showed up.

"Well?" the newcomer demanded. "How did it go?"

"I think he'll show up for the card game, Mister Luther. But the truth is, I don't like this much."

"You don't have to like it. You're being paid not to like nor to dislike, but simply to do a job." As he said that Tandy Luther was counting out the gold money which he handed the mate. "Any questions?"

"No, Mister Luther, no questions," Trumpy said reluctantly.

He watched as Luther strode off up the deck and then turned to the rail, watching night settle over the Missouri, watching the dark water slip by the hull of the *Alabama Maid*.

Shelter awakened to the rolling of the steamboat—he guess they were making a bend in the river, since that was the only time he felt any movement on this big flat-bottomed vessel.

He stretched and sat up in the dark cabin. The nap had refreshed him a little. There were still a few hours to make up for after the long trail from Wyoming.

Glancing out the porthole he saw a star drifting through a veil of cloud. Shell yawned, lit the lantern and examined himself in the mirror. He still had most of that shave, and he decided against a fresh one. He splashed a little water on his hair and wiped it back.

He had decided to take Trumpy up on his offer. There was nothing else to do but walk the decks. Frowning, he looked his fresh shirt over—it was fresh compared to his trail shirt, but the dark blue material was wrinkled some, and it was getting thin on the cuffs. It would have to do. He had only his sheepskin jacket and so he would wear no coat. After trying to brush his hat clean, he decided to go hatless as well, although that was almost painful. His Colt he wore.

Going out he locked the door and slipped the key into his pocket. The night was warm, the sky dark, moonless. The banks were rife with willow and scrub oak. The murmuring of frogs was constant as they drifted down the dark river.

On the deck he met ladies and gentlemen moving the same direction he was. They were sporting fresh suits and fancy gowns and for a moment Shelter hesitated. He didn't like feeling out of place, and it was obvious he would be.

"Wondered if you were coming," Trumpy said, approaching him from the shadows.

"Yeah, I'm coming," Shelter decided. "For a while at least."

"Good." Trumpy put a familiar hand on Shelter's shoulder—a gesture Shell didn't quite like. Together then they walked to the main dining room which was awash with light.

A string quartet played softly on a stage, glasses tinkled and quiet laughter filled the room. Ladies in their finery and jewels sat to the tables where faro was being dealt. Along one wall was a buffet table with food and wine.

Trumpy escorted Shell to the table, bowing to one passenger and another. There was smoked tongue, cheese, rice and barbecued beef. Farther along was ham and duck, fresh bread and a huge salad.

Shell filled his plate and accepted a glass of port from Trumpy. Then he stood near the wall, watching the people. Some he watched more closely than others.

She was there—the woman from the deck. She had changed her dress and was wearing white satin and lace. Her throat and shoulders were incredibly white, smooth, alluring. The earrings she wore caught the light and sparkled brilliantly.

She had not changed expression, however, and with those dark, haughty eyes she surveyed Shelter Morgan across the room, saying something in a low voice to the man beside

40

her, a tall gent who sported a narrow mustache.

Shell turned his back and walked to another table, watching the betting on a fast round of faro. Only now and then did he glance back toward the woman in white satin; and twice when he did, she was gazing back.

"He is the one?" the lady in white satin asked the man beside her. "You are sure, are you, Luther?"

"I'm sure, Alexandra," Tandy Luther answered. He sipped at his wine and lifted his eyes to Shelter Morgan who had his back to them at the moment.

"It's a shame," Alexandra sighed. She let her eyes linger on the tall man, noting the broad shoulders, the slim hips, the easy way he moved. "But if it has to be done . . ."

"We can't let him get to New Orleans," Tandy said.

"Well then, what must be done must be done." Alexandra tasted her own wine and added, "Still it is a shame."

At that moment Shelter turned toward her as if he had felt her eyes on him, and their eyes met. Alexandra smiled, faintly, and she saw his answering smile. Then she turned her eyes away, returning her attention to the faro game.

Shell finished his plate and refilled his wine glass from the decanter. He wandered through the dining room watching the card players, listening to the music. When he looked back to where the woman in white had been sitting, he found that she was gone.

There was nothing else to stay around for and so after finishing his port Shelter walked out into the cool evening. A nighthawk cut a fleeting silhouette against the late rising moon and the grumbling of the frogs along the banks set up a primitive counterpoint to the music drifting from the dining room.

Shelter walked to the stern, enjoying the cool air, the quiet evening. He watched the wake the steamboat cut against the dark river and lifted his eyes to a distant yellow light, the only light visible along the shore.

The sound of approaching footsteps brought his head around.

It was already too late. They were on him in a rush out of the darkness. They swarmed over Shelter with fists and clubs and he fought back desperately.

Shelter shot out a straight right and saw a white head snap back, but a club landed on his shoulder just beside his neck and the pain shot through him.

Angrily he kicked out and caught someone's leg. A fist slammed into his ribs, knocking the breath from him and a second blow caught him flush on the jaw.

Shelter threw up a shielding forearm which just deflected a heavy club. With lefts and rights he swung out furiously, catching a man coming in on the temple.

He tried to duck away, to move along the rail, but it was hopeless. They battered him with fists and feet and he could do nothing but curl up in a ball, lashing out with his fists.

Shelter brought up a knee, catching a thug in the groin and the man howled with pain. Then he saw the club overhead begin a vicious downward arc and he felt it thud against his skull, filling him with numbing pain. He staggered and started to go down and he felt their hands on him.

He tried to fight them off, but it was useless. He felt the dizzy spinning in his head, the hot pain along his ribcage. Then the hands lifted him high and he was thrown over the rail, narrowly missing the blades of the mammoth sternwheeler's paddle as he plunged into the icy, black water below.

Gasping for breath Shelter fought his way to the surface, watching as the *Alabama Maid* made her placid way downriver, the music from her dining room lingering in the air, her sternwheel churning the water to white briefly in passing before the river and the night settled to blackness.

It was a good hundred yards to shore and Shelter's head was throbbing. A nausea swept through his body and he felt as if he were going to black out. Desperately he swam toward the shore, wanting to make it before he did go under.

His arms were wooden, his legs dead, sensationless, and his heart was pounding like a hundred hammers. Shell stroked toward the distant shoreline, barely able to make it out, black against the black of the water in the night.

The frogs continued their ceaseless chorus, and now it seemed mocking to Shelter's ears. His dizziness was deeper now and the pain surged through him with each stroke of his battered arms. His lungs burned with fiery need and Shelter could feel his strength waning by the moment.

The current swept him downriver, and actually towed him back toward midstream where the current was quickest. The *Maid* was gone around a bend in the river and everything was dark, silent but for the lights exploding in Shelter's head, the constant grumping of the frogs, the desperate splashing Shell's arms made against the water.

He was still being swept downstream, more rapidly it seemed, and for every stroke he took toward the receding shore, he moved a stroke downriver.

His arms moved woodenly, mechanically, and with a shock of realization he was suddenly aware that his mouth was filled with water, that his swimming was only a feeble, nearly futile gesture against the inevitability of drowning.

Shelter shook off that bleak thought and willed his arms to move, willed his legs to kick out in defiance. He could will it, but he could not will away the ringing in his ears, the blinding flashes of light, the waves of nausea.

His arms were no longer moving, but Shelter was not aware of it. The water was cold, but that no longer bothered him. He simply drifted in the current, unaware of the river or the night. He simply floated and the night went silent.

It was Doggett who spotted it first. Holding the lantern aloft he peered into the rushes.

"What is it?" Jackson Turner wanted to know.

"Hell, ain't nothin' worth a damn," Doggett called back. "Only a dead man."

Jackson Turner came to his feet and walked the length of the raft, going to where Andy Doggett held the lantern illuminating the reeds and cattails.

He glanced down, "Sure as hell is a man. He don't stink."

"Not yet. He ain't even stiff. Might've fell off that steamboat."

"Haul him on board," Turner said abruptly. Jackson Turner simply blinked at him, his narrow, bearded face cocked off to one side.

"He's dead, Jackson," Doggett said. "A dead man ain't worth much."

"Sometimes yes, sometimes no," Jackson Turner replied impatiently. "Let's have us a look in his pockets."

Together they dragged the limp body from the cold Missouri, and they laid it down on the raft, hanging the lantern on the mast overhead.

Jackson got to his knees and patted the pockets and then he frowned, stopping his search suddenly.

"What's the matter?"

"He ain't dead," Jackson answered.

"He what?"

"He ain't dead yet. Get me a pole, Andy."

"What for?" the riverman asked. His larger partner turned toward him, his face washed with lanternlight.

"What the hell you think for! He ain't dead."

"There ain't no need to do that," Andy Doggett protested.

Jackson Turner's jaw tightened visibly; he was not used to having Doggett back talk him. "If he comes around he'll likely put the blame on us. Even sayin' he doesn't, that makes us nursemaids. I don't want to fool with the man, Andy. I plain don't want the problems a live man presents."

"All right. Well . . . all right," Doggett said nervously, "Just go through his pockets then —what size are them boots?—and we'll roll him back into the water, all right? No need to cave his skull in."

Turner was already into the pockets, but he found nothing at all but a small pen knife. They pulled his boots off, but found them too large for both of them.

"Wasn't worth fishing him out," Turner growled.

Doggett sagged down on a barrel and watched as Turner sorted out the thoughts in his mind, trying to find some way to salvage the effort they had expended.

When Shelter's eyes flickered open he saw

them over him. A wide shouldered man with red hair and a torn shirt and a smaller man with a weasel's face, a scattering of whiskers and a stupid expression. The big man nudged his partner.

"Now look, Doggett. He's comin' around."

Shelter tried to sit up, found he could not, and turned his head, coughing up the water which had gotten into his lungs.

He felt battered and torn, and the breathing was difficult. He managed to turn his head back toward the two river rats.

"Thanks," he said. "I was done if you hadn't pulled me out."

They did not answer immediately. A white moon drifted across the sky, glossing the Missouri. The willows moved in the light breeze.

"Well." Jackson Turner hovered over Shell, "And what is your life worth?" he asked.

"To me?" Shell attempted a smile. "I'll repay you," he promised.

"When? "

"As soon as I'm able. If you could take me to the next town downriver . . . "

"You got money there?" Turner demanded.

"I'm headin' for New Orleans . . . "

"Swimmin' there, was you? " Doggett laughed.

"I was on the steamboat. I got thrown off." Shell looked from one man to the other, not liking what he saw now. The narrow one looked dim as a candle under a bushel basket, the big one plain mean.

47

"I don't know how," Shelter told them with sincerity, "but I'll pay you back for pulling me out."

"I don't know how either," Jackson Turner said. "But you damned sure will."

What Turner meant by that Shell couldn't puzzle out, perhaps the man didn't know himself. Shelter liked none of this but he could hardly sit up let alone take a chance on swimming the river again and so he closed his eyes, letting the cold and damp envelop him as he slept a troubled sleep.

It was chill, hardly gray in the east when Shell was nudged roughly awake by Jackson Turner's boot toe.

"Get up," he snarled.

He hadn't the strength to argue and so, hanging on to the rough mast he dragged himself to his feet. Turner watched him sourly. A low winging flight of ducks skimmed across the Missouri. The sun was painting the eastern skies red now. The bottoms were dark and chill, a thin fog drifting across the oxbow where the raft was tied up.

"Hell, this ain't never gonna work," Doggett muttered with disgust. "Look at him, he can't hardly stand."

"He'll get his strength back. He'd better."

"What's this about?" Shell wanted to know.

"Well it's like this," Jackson Turner said, drawing it out, enjoying himself. "You are a southbound man but this here—this is a north-bound raft. We been poling upriver for four days. Truth is, we're damned tired of it."

Shelter got the idea. He started forward angrily, but pulled up short catching sight of the musket in Doggett's fists. The little man was perched on a barrel, with the muzzle of that ancient weapon trained on Morgan.

"So I'm the labor force," Shell said.

"That's it. You ain't dumb, are you, partner?" Turner looped a rope around Shelter's neck while Doggett covered him. There was a hangman's knot in that line and he cinched it down around Shelter's throat.

"It won't be so bad," Turner said, but Shelter didn't find much assurance in that. "You see, the way we figure it you'd be dead by now, wasn't for us. So you owe us. Now you can do us this favor and when we hit Biddleton, why we'll cut you loose. We'll all be square."

"I can't go back upriver," Shell exploded, but Turner yanked the noose and he slacked off.

"You gonna have to go back upriver, boy! It's that or take a dive back into the big Mo . . . with a little lead to weight you down."

4.

The day which had been chilly had grown incredibly hot. The air was muggy, breathless along the banks of the Missouri.

Shelter labored beneath the sun, the eyes of the river rats. The noose was around his neck, the other end hitched to the mast.

With a twenty foot pole Shelter pushed the raft upriver. Planting it, then walking the length of the raft, fighting the river twenty feet at a time. His legs were still badly bruised, his arms knotted, his shirt in tatters.

Doggett sat on a barrel, back against the mast, musket in his hands. Jackson Turner lounged across the rudder, his hat pulled low, sucking a straw as he watched the sweat rain off Shelter, watched his muscles bunch and strain as he poled that rickety raft against the current.

By noon Shelter was a zombie moving up and down the raft without thought or awareness. Turner and Doggett shared a meal of tinned beef and beans. None was offered to Shelter, and he knew it was useless to ask.

They did not care if he lived or died. They were rested now and if Shelter should drop dead they would simply overboard him and continue on their way.

But Shelter would not die. He worked through a haze of exhaustion, seeing nothing but the water, the raft beneath his feet. And all the while he was moving away from New Orleans, all the time Roland Blue was getting farther out of reach.

Who had had him beaten, thrown overboard? There was no answer to that which Shell could find. Perhaps a member of the circus troupe, trailing behind . . . but how would anyone other than Blue know who he was?

It was a puzzle and with his mind whirring, with the exhaustion of his body, the hot sun beating down, he could not even frame the question correctly, let alone find the elusive answer.

As Shelter watched, the water grew darker and his head snapped up, his red-rimmed eyes going to the sky. It was nearly dark already, but how? The hours which had been so long, eternal, had suddenly been swept away by onrushing darkness.

Now they would have to stop, sleep . . . was there anything more desirable than sleep?

And then what?

He already knew the answer. Tomorrow would bring the same. The endless walking, the pushing, the heat. And there would be no food again. They would work Shelter until he could no longer work. Then they would let him die.

If he let them—but he swore then he would not. Now, while he still had a fraction of his strength, he must make a move, even if it ended in sudden death. He would not go out like a dog.

Gradually, he hoped imperceptibly, Shelter slowed his pace, trying to gather his strength. The orange-tinted clouds hovered above the western horizon. The land was going dark.

"Look for a place to put in," he heard Jackson tell Doggett. The little man stretched and rose to his feet.

Shelter was at the back of the raft, just finishing his round and as Doggett stood, peering at the shoreline Shelter lifted that pole and swung out with all his might.

Dogget shouted and then splashed into the

water, the musket falling from his hands. Shelter dropped the pole and tore at the noose around his neck, but Jackson Turner was already on him, throwing two hard right hand hooks against Shell's jaw. Shelter struck back savagely, but he could not fight and untie the noose at the same time.

Doggett was paddling in the water, yelling his head off, and Turner who was stronger than Shell had suspected was still throwing punches at Shell. A wild right glanced off of Shelter's skull but a stiff left from Turner caught him flush and set the bells to ringing.

Shelter staggered back, teetered on the edge of the raft and then fell, a flurry of punches from Jackson Turner chasing him.

Shell splashed back, plunging under the dark skin of the Missouri and Jackson Turner, fists still clenched stood there, watching the ripples, the bubbles.

"Jackson! Jackson!" Doggett was calling for help, but Jackson Turner paid him no mind. All of his attention was on the spot where Morgan had gone in.

A slow, vicious smile crossed Jackson Turner's lips and he bent down, picking up the rope. With a violent tug he yanked on the line. But it was slack and it came to him.

Cursing, Jackson Turner hauled the line up, finding the empty noose on the end of the wet rope.

"Jackson!" Doggett was still calling for

help, but his voice was farther away as the raft drifted with the current.

Turner held the noose limply, searching the dark river. Then he heard the sound behind him and he spun.

It was already too late. Shelter Morgan had that rain barrel high overhead and as Turner spun toward him he let go, bringing it down with all of his strength and it caught Turner full in the chest, slamming him from the raft into the dark river with a splash, a groan and a following violent curse.

Shelter stood on the raft, his arms dangling, his shirt torn, his clothing soaked through. Doggett's head bobbed near the shore, and closer to him an insanely angry Jackson Turner.

"I'll get you!" Turner took a few swimming strokes after the raft. But it was already into the current, slipping inexorably away from Turner, and he could see the swimming was futile.

He raised a fist from the water and screamed again, "I'll find you! I'll kill you!"

But the current was swift, the river wide and already Jackson Turner was far behind, his threats fading to whispers as Shelter Morgan sagged to the deck of the raft, watching the shoreline slip steadily past.

He drifted through the night and for three days after. There was a bit of food on board and a fishing line which Shell used with good success. Turner and Doggett had a small, jerry-built stove as well, and Shelter floated lazily downriver, the good smells of fish frying mingled with the fresh river air. He lay flat on his back, shirtless, taking in the warm sunshine.

Hurrying was useless and so he did not attempt it. He let the river take its course, let nature heal his body and return his strength.

On the second day he made the big bend at Saint Louis, swinging into the broad Mississippi. There was a deal of traffic on the river, but Shelter stayed near the middle and was able to steer past although a big sidewheeler threatened to swamp him, its whistle blasting a warning.

He hit New Orleans sunburned, bearded, half-naked. He was broke, weaponless and alone. He intended to let none of that slow him down.

The wharves were busy with ships unloading cotton, tobacco, indigo and rice. On the gulf side clippers off loaded tea and silks, china and lacquer goods from the Orient. All along the quays keelboats handled by shouting, big shouldered men, transferred bales of furs and buffalo hides to the wagons onshore as buyers with sheets of paper in hand scurried from one vessel to the next.

Shell nudged his raft into a piling under a mossy pier and tied it up. There was a rotting ladder running up to the plank deck of the pier and he climbed up emerging from the shadows into the bright Louisiana sunlight, hatless, bootless, shirtless among the busy dockworkers who scarcely spared him a glance as they moved their heavy carts along the wharf.

"Seen a circus?" Shelter asked the nearest man.

The teamster eyed Shelter thoughtfully, with amusement. "No, but don't worry, they'll wait for you. I'd reckon you're the main attraction, Mister." Then he laughed out loud and Shelter had to grin in return.

He had no money and no clothes. Yet he did have one idea and he walked the docks until he found the steamboat line.

Shelter pushed open the office door and walked in, past the ticket buying customers, the shipping merchants. A woman turned her head aside as he strode to the counter.

"What in hell . . . ?" the clerk looked up at the shirtless, sunburned man before him. He was about to order him out, but those cool blue eyes gave him pause to consider it twice. "What is it you want?"

"I'm just another satisfied customer," Shelter said. "My name's Morgan, I had a ticket down on the *Alabama Maid*."

"The *Alabama* . . . Morgan! Yes, yes." The clerk scratched his head. "I recall now. It was presumed that you were dead. There was even an article in the newspaper."

A second man, wearing a dark blue suit had appeared from the inner office. His eyes opened wide and his lips turned down when he spotted Shell.

"Mister Langdon," the clerk said, "this is Morgan—off the *Alabama Maid*."

"Morgan . . . ?" the man's face clouded and then cleared abruptly. "Come into my office. Come in, Sir," Langdon told Shell.

Shelter followed him into a cozy office which was panelled with mahogany and hung with paintings of ships.

"Sit down," Langdon told Shell. "George!" he called through a side door, "come in here."

"You've been through a lot, it seems," Langdon said, sitting to his desk. "I am sorry."

"I don't blame the line."

"No, but other people might. It's not good publicity to have people disappearing off our ships. I assume you've come for your belongings."

"That's right. If you've still got them."

A narrow, blond haired kid had appeared in the office. "George," Langdon said, "get down to lost and found and pick up Morgan's belongings. I hope . . . you have everything you need in there."

"I doubt that. If I recall I had a shirt and my coat. And my hat and rifle. But as you can see . . . " Shelter held up a bare foot.

"I see. And your horse . . . it would have been boarded at Stacy's. It should be there if it hasn't been sold. If it has, the line will replace it."

The kid had returned with Shelter's saddlebags, his coat and Winchester. Shell dug right into the bags and pulled out that wrinkled red shirt, putting it on. He also planted his hat on his head.

"I'm terribly sorry," Langdon repeated.

Shell lifted a hand. "Like I say, I don't blame the line. But it does leave me unshod."

"Yes. I can see that." Langdon smiled briefly and then lifted a strongbox from his bottom drawer. Opening it he withdrew a small sack of gold coins. "Your horse—you'll have to pay for his board. Your boots, of course, and . . . "

"A Colt revolver and holster," Shell finished.

Langdon nodded and counted out four gold eagles. "If this will satisfy you?" he asked hopefully.

"Absolutely, Mister Langdon, and I appreciate your attitude." Shell stood, hefting his rifle and saddlebags. "Now there's just two things. Number one, can you have that young man show me where the stable is?"

"Certainly. And the other item?"

"Is there a circus in town?"

"A . . . " Langdon's face was puzzled, but he answered, "Why, yes—that is, there was. They're gone now. Into Texas, I believe. Was there some . . . ?"

But the tall man had already risen, and with a nod he was out the door, following the kid up the cobblestone road to the stable on Montague Boulevard.

The black was there, and it lifted its head in recognition as Shelter went to the stall.

"Nice looking animal," the stableman said, "I had a buyer all ready."

Shell patted the big black's neck and asked, "You've got my saddle and gear too? "

"Sure have. Now after what you've been through, I hate to charge you for the feed, but it does cost money, you know."

"That's all right."

He wanted four dollars which left Shelter with plenty. There was a gunshop not two blocks from the stable and Shelter went in, still barefoot and picked out a new, sweet-actioned Colt. "I'll need a hundred rounds or so, too," he told the owner of the shop.

"A hundred? Planning on a lot of practice or starting a war."

"Maybe both." Shell had selected a holster as well, one with plenty of cutaway around the trigger. He could devise a thong for rough country out of a piggin string later.

Satisfied with his purchase he walked uptown through the carts and flower ladies, the gambling men and musicians of the French Quarter until he found a boot shop.

"No need to ask what you want," the Frenchman there said with a smile. "Look around, if you don't see what you want, ask."

Shell picked out a sturdy, unornamented pair of rough cuts and paid ten dollars for them. Then, feeling alive and equipped once again he searched out a hotel.

There was a wait while they cleaned up a room for him, and Shelter began going through the stack of newspapers in the lobby until he found what he was looking for.

The item was ten days old:

After a successful engagement in New Orleans, the Roland Blue Circus today packed up its tents and rolled out for a tour of the state of Texas, beginning with a three-week stay in the city of Houston . . .

Houston. Shelter folded the paper and replaced it. If Blue actually stayed there for three weeks then Shelter would catch up before they had moved on again.

Yet something about this did not feel right to Shelter. Blue was covering a lot of ground quickly. His stay in New Orleans couldn't have been a long one. And now Houston—why, with all the opportunities the nearer cities provided?

Shelter knew nothing about travelling shows, but he had the idea they usually hit most of the large towns, travelling slowly. Blue was hitting widely separated towns and moving fast.

He lay on his hotel bed still thinking on that as night fell over New Orleans. Thinking of that and of other things. He still wondered who had thrown him from the *Alabama Maid* and why.

One last thought crossed his mind before he fell off to sleep and he lay there in the dark thinking of that beautiful, haughty woman in white satin.

5.

The sky above was a deep, clouded red above the blue-black of the sea when Shelter Morgan rode out of New Orleans. Back in the hotel dining room he had heard talk of a hurricane moving into the gulf. Just now it was sultry, the air utterly calm.

Shell felt fine. He had a good horse, a good gun, and a spare ten dollars. The road was straight and deeply rutted, lined with ancient magnolia trees on the sea side.

The sun was hot on Shelter's back and his shirt stuck to him. There was little traffic on the road and few farms. The few there were dwindled to nothing as he drifted into the lowland marshes.

It was still hot in the bayous, but the thick vegetation cut out the light and the day grew dark as Shelter wound through the cypress forests, hearing muskrat and otter splash into the water at his approach. Twice he saw gators.

The going was boggy, the air alive with mosquitoes. Across the deeper bogs, planking or logs had been laid at sometime in the past.

He saw no one except a suspicious Cajun and once a swamp Indian who disappeared like a shadow into the bayous.

The days continued sultry, breathless. The sun dawned red each morning. Finding the Sabine three days later was a blessing. Some folks, he supposed, liked that bayou country, but Shelter was not one of them. Now he had Texas across the river.

The ferryman gave him a dollar's worth of ride across the Sabine and fifty dollars worth of jawing.

"Houston, is it?" the boatman asked. "Well, that's all right, I suppose, but I never favored it myself. Now Fort Worth—there's a friendly town. Had me a woman once in Fort Worth. She could bake peach turnovers like nothin' you ever did taste. But Houston's all right, I suppose—but I wouldn't travel no farther west just now. The Comanche are kicking up something fierce west of the Brazos."

Shelter nodded, tried to look interested and watched the river drift past, his eyes on the Texas bank of the Sabine. It was less than a hundred miles to Houston, and with luck he was closing the gap rapidly on the murderer who ran ahead of him.

"You see them red skies this morning," the ferryman continued as he tied up at the far shore, "now that's a warning to you. Anybody spent much time around this Gulf Coast knows there's a big one blowin' up out at sea. A hurry-cane, now if you never seen that, you've never seen weather . . . "

"I appreciate the ride. And the advice." Shelter shook the man's hand and rode off, leaving the man to his lonely job, awaiting the next unlucky passenger.

The land was gradually rising, and now there was a cooling breeze as evening crept in across the empty land. Shelter rode until full dark, not wanting to waste a minute of daylight.

He camped on a small, barren knoll, his back to the rising wind, drinking coffee while the horse grazed on the sparse buffalo grass, while the stars blinked on one by one. There were times Shelter wondered about the sort of life he led, the sort of man he had become, and tonight was one of those times.

Alone in an empty land, with no company

but his horse, his only goal a bloody meeting with a butcher. Other men were in their own houses now, with a woman puttering around the kitchen, with a comfortable bed waiting.

But then other men hadn't seen their friends cut down in ambush, seen the needless bloodshed in the final moments of a bloody war, watched as men he had taken for friends and comrades grimly opened fire on them for the sake of that gold.

A star fell across the skies and Shelter watched its brief, brilliant flight. Then he tossed the dregs of his coffee into the fire and rolled up, chasing the doubts from his mind with sleep.

With the dawn he was riding westward again, and he stayed in the saddle for long hours, stopping only when the big black gelding appeared to need rest. He passed a deserted farm and an entire town which had been burned to the ground; on the morning of the third day he sat on a low ridge looking over Houston.

Shelter stepped down from the black and squatted on his heels, watching. Off to the north was the old fort, and to the south the blue ribbon of the sea. Across the town were the cattle pens, half full. And just on the outskirts the circus tents were pitched.

This was it then. He would wait until dark and then ride in. Shelter removed the saddle from the black and let it roll in the grass. Then, leaning up against the lone oak he spread out a blanket and cleaned and oiled his guns, watching the brightly colored pennants which flew from the circus tents. Watching, waiting until dark.

As sundown crept across the plains, the lights began to flicker on across Houston. The circus was brightly lit and now Shelter could see folks drifting toward it on horseback, afoot or in their surreys.

He stood, stretched and saddled the black. It was odd but he felt no excitement. Maybe it was simply that he had been chasing Blue for so long it seemed unreal. He favored these periods of calm. Losing his temper had landed him in trouble a time or two. The man who can keep his head in a dangerous situation always has the edge.

Shelter stepped into leather, the saddle creaking beneath him. Then he kneed the black forward, coming down off that ridge and into Houston as darkness settled.

The huffing music of a calliope drifted through the air as Shelter hit the circus grounds. They were crowded with customers and from within the big tent a roar of appreciation went up.

Shelter paid his quarter and went on in, shouldering through the crowd as he looked for the owner's wagon. The crowd thinned as he worked his way around to the back of the big tent, startling two kids who were trying to slip under the canvas.

Two clowns, half his size walked past, one of them smoking a cigar, and from a ways farther back he heard the chilling roar of a big cat.

The wagons were parked all in a row, decorated with gilt curlicues and crimson lettering. Shelter smiled as he caught sight of a painting of an acrobatic troupe on the white wagon beside him. The girl, in red underwear, floated through the air while a man in white waited to catch her. Looking at that costume it was no wonder the kid in KC had been sparked.

Shell stopped in the shadows, hearing voices.

"All right! All right!"

There was something else said, but Shelter could make nothing out of it. From a dark blue wagon a man emerged, the shaft of light from the open door cutting a rectangle against the packed earth of the yard.

Shell tugged his hat low and walked slowly forward, reading the sign on the wagon door —"Manager."

The door was still slowly swinging closed when Shelter hit it with his shoulder and it banged open. Shell stood in the dimly lit wagon, fists clenched facing a man across a desk, a man he had never seen before.

"Who are you? Get the hell out of here!"

He was a man of middle years with a bull neck and wide shoulders. He wore his shirt sleeves rolled up as he went through the papers on his desk.

"I'm looking for Roland Blue," Shelter said.

"He ain't here," the man growled.

"Where is he?"

"He ain't here, damnit! Now get the hell out of my office."

Shell stepped forward, leaning across the desk. He yanked the big man to his feet by his shirt front and held him there, eye to eye.

"I asked you a question. I asked politely."

The man blinked, his face reddening. A shadow fell across the desk and Shelter knew there was another man in the room. He threw the big man aside and ducked just as an axe handle thudded past his ear and slammed into the desk.

Shell turned and caught the man with the club by the forearm. Yanking down hard he bent the arm across his knee until he heard the crack of bone and the scream of pain.

Throwing the injured man aside, Shelter turned back toward the desk and found himself looking into the twin, cavernous muzzles of a ten-gauge shotgun. The big man behind the triggers was not smiling.

"You asked me a question, and I answered," he told Shell. "Then I asked you to leave— and *I* asked politely. Now I'm through with politeness."

He drew back those twin hammers and Shelter saw a light in the man's eyes he did not like. He was sure he was going to pull those triggers.

"What's the problem, Ed?" the voice at Shelter's shoulder interrupted.

It was a woman's voice and Shell turned slowly toward her, his hands raised. She was young and beautiful, with red hair cascading across her shoulders. She wore only a white dressing gown.

"This man busted in here, Hope. Looking for Blue."

"He did?" the woman's voice was puzzled. The man in the corner was slumped to the floor, moaning as he cradled his broken arm. "Just what did you want to see Mister Blue about?" she asked Shelter.

"I'd sooner talk to him face to face," Shell said, careful not to move too quickly with that scattergun trained on him.

"That's not possible. Mister Blue has gone ahead in advance of the circus, arranging bookings."

"He wouldn't listen," the big man said disgustedly.

"But perhaps if you told me what it is you want," the red haired woman said. Her eyes were a deep green, her complexion very light with here and there a freckle.

"I'd like a job," Shell told her.

"A job!" she laughed aloud. "This is a fine way to apply."

"Things kind of got out of hand," Shelter grinned.

"So I see—are you all right, Danny?" she asked the injured man.

"I've got a broken arm," the man answered. He looked at the arm in bewilderment.

68

"Well, I guess we might as well hire you on," the woman said.

"Now wait a damned minute, Hope," the big man exploded. "After this . . . ?"

"Why not?" she asked with a smile. "He's obviously strong. And, it does seem we're short a roustabout now."

The big man's eyes flickered to the corner where Danny still sat, moaning. He shook his head in disgust and slowly lowered the shotgun, carefully letting the hammers down.

"You know I won't argue with you, Hope," the big man said, "but it's damned foolish."

"Yes." She looked Shelter up and down, her green eyes sparkling. "I suppose it is, but it won't be the first foolish thing I've done."

Outside it was still warm. The rising moon was silver above the circus tent. Shelter and Hope stopped in the shadows and Shell told her, "Thanks for helping me out in there. I had the notion the big man was going to shoot."

"He might have. Ed is quick-tempered and mean."

Her green eyes reflected the moonlight and Shelter's eyes lingered there, then dropped to her breasts which were full, straining against the white silk of her dressing gown.

"When do you expect Mister Blue might be back?" Shell asked.

"Blue? You've got your job, Mister . . ."

"Jones," Shell smiled.

"You've got your job, Mister Jones."

69

"I'd still like to talk to him."

"I'm not sure . . . a few days, I suppose." Hope answered. There was curiosity in her eyes now. Shell read that there and decided not to push it for now.

"Where do I sleep?" he asked.

"Around the other side you'll find a red wagon with yellow trim. That's the roustabouts wagon. You can find a bunk there. For now." She smiled, just faintly and she looked into Shelter's eyes. "Maybe later we can find more comfortable accommodations."

"I *am* a comfort loving man," Shell said. They stood near together, so near that neither could move without touching the other. Shelter watched those starlit, promising eyes a long moment longer.

"I'm not sure I'm doing you a favor, letting you stay," Hope warned him. "Ed will hold a grudge—you can count on it. Danny was popular with the men, too. It would be a lot safer for you if you simply rode out now."

"Safer, maybe. But I'd hate to think I might be missing out on some comfort, Hope."

"Yes." She studied the tall man again, carefully, and she nodded slowly. "I would hate to think that too. Just be careful, Mister . . . Jones."

Then Shelter touched his hat brim and turned, walking away. Hope drew her wrapper more tightly around her, watching him go. She smiled and then concern crossed her expression, and she turned, walking slowly back toward her wagon.

"That's trouble there, Miss Hope," Ed said, coming out of the shadows.

"Yes, I guess it is."

"Are you sure you know what you're doing?"

"No, Ed. I'm not. I'm not sure at all."

Applause erupted in the main tent as Shelter reached his horse. The show had ended, and the spectators trickled slowly out of the tent as Shell led the black around to the rear of the circus grounds.

The wagon wasn't hard to find and Shelter went up to it as a man and a woman led a trio of caparisoned elephants past. There was one man inside. He looked up sleepily from the worn deck of cards he was shuffling. A hollow-eyed, pale man, he had the look of a drinker about him.

"Name's Jones," Shell said. "I was told to find a bunk here."

Without speaking the man lifted a pointing finger. Shell followed it with his eyes and then walked to the bunk, throwing his saddlebags on it.

He pulled off his shirt and propped himself up against the wall, hands behind his head, watching the thin man play solitaire.

He had just managed to get comfortable when the door slapped open and a trio of roustabouts came in. Rugged, thick shoul-dered men they were and their leader had an ugly scowl as he looked at Shelter.

"You Jones?" he asked.

"That's right."

"You ain't wanted. Get out."

"Sorry," Shelter answered. "I'm here to stay."

The big man's jaw twitched and he took a step toward Shelter. Then he stopped. "You might be here," he muttered, "but you damn sure aren't stayin'. Not after what you done to Danny."

Then, mumbling, he turned away the others watching. They sat to the table, sharing a bottle of whisky while Shelter watched. When they looked his way, there was sullen anger in their eyes.

He wondered if it was Danny's broken arm that had them fired up or Ed's encouragement. He would have bet it was the latter.

The big man, whose name was McGinnis, got up and turned the lamp down, standing for a moment in the open door. Shelter unfolded the worn blanket which was on the foot of the bed and pulled it over him, tilting his hat down low across his eyes.

He heard the men moving around, undressing and crawling into their bunks, and then the lamp was blown out.

Shelter lay there in the silence, trying to sort things out. The long trail was ended; he had found the circus. But he had come in with a bang and a flash and that might prove dangerous.

Now and then he thought of the incident

72

on the steamboat, of that woman in white satin, but it was all so distant from Blue and Texas that it seemed unreal. Why then did it plague him, nagging at his thoughts?

He also wondered where Blue really was. Scouting the route ahead, arranging bookings —was that the owner's job? He gave thought to all of that, but he did not dwell on it. None of it mattered as long as he found Blue and put the fear of God in him . . . Shelter heard a floorboard squeak and beneath the blanket he drew back the hammer of that Colt.

The sound was loud, menacing in the night and the floorboard squeaked again as whoever it had been moved back away from Shelter Morgan's bunk.

6.

Shelter rolled out with the rest of the crew at first light. The skies at dawning still held that reddish, threatening glow.

Breakfast was at a long plank table in a small tent. Hotcakes and bacon which Shelter ate silently. No one ventured a word to him but for one angular Swede who noticed Shell's gun and said, "You won't need that, Jones."

"I wouldn't bet on it," he answered.

With the tents set up already the roustabouts work was clean-up. Shelter was given the new hand's work—shovelling the elephant's pen out.

From the looks of the pen it hadn't been cleaned since the circus hit Houston. With a shovel and wheelbarrow he got to it, laboring under the warm morning sun.

From time to time he looked the elephants over. He had never been side by side with a creature that could crush him to dust. The big one, Nancy as they called her, had a shoulder so high that Shell had to stretch his arm out to full length just to touch it.

Yet they were placid enough and Shelter managed to make friends with them like you would with a horse, by offering them wisps of hay.

"I see you got the greenhorn's job."

Shelter looked up to see Hope outside the rope. He smiled and shrugged.

"Well, I am a greenhorn at this."

Hope's eyes lingered on his broad, bare chest, those wide shoulders.

"But I imagine you've had some practice at other kinds of work."

"Some." Shell leaned on his shovel, a faint smile dancing across his lips.

"Which makes me wonder—why'd a grown-up boy like you decide to run away from home and take up with a circus?"

"Well," he said soberly, "I've always kind of had this sense of adventure."

"If that's your kind of adventure . . . "

Hope looked from Shelter to the elephants and they both laughed. "Look . . . Jones, why don't you come by for lunch? You know where my wagon is? I can promise you better than you'll get from Cooky."

"I'd be obliged," Shelter said.

"Good . . . for lunch then."

Shelter looked up from his down-slanted hat and nodded, watching as Hope walked away, those full, fluid hips holding his attention.

"Taking care of the girls, are you?"

"What?" Shelter turned to find a small, swarthy man of twenty or so behind him.

"My girls." The circus man grinned and waved a hand around him, indicating the elephants.

"I've been trying," Shell replied.

He watched for a minute as the elephant trainer walked around Nancy, examining her. Then he slipped the elephant a treat from his pocket, and when she had popped in into her mouth and extended her trunk for seconds, the little man instead took the trunk, patted it twice and turned around.

As gently as a mother Nancy coiled that trunk around him and picked him up, placing him on her back.

The elephant trainer grabbed her ear and turned her. "Time for a little exercise," he called down to Shell and slapping Nancy's ear he got her into slow motion; the other elephants automatically followed. The trainer led them down into the creek bottom where they drank and sprayed themselves with water.

Shell watched for a minute, shaking his head in wonder. Then he got back to his work. It was hard, messy, but he was making progress. He minded it not at all despite the strong smells —it had been some time since he had worked in the sun, using those shoulder and back muscles and it felt fine to stretch them out a little.

Near noon Shelter saw the other roustabouts going toward the chow tent, although no one had bothered to tell him it was lunch time. So he leaned his shovel up against a post and walked back toward his wagon, wanting his soap, needing to wash up a little before dining with a lady.

There was no one in the wagon, for which Shelter was grateful and he walked to his bunk. His saddlebags, he saw immediately, had been moved slightly and his blanket had been unfolded.

Shaking his head, Shelter picked up the blanket.

It came instantly to life. A large flat-headed snake which had been asleep beneath the blanket reared its head. There was no time for considering. Shelter had never seen a cobra before, but that hooded head looked venomous, deadly and even as he watched it struck, with incredible swiftness.

Yet Shelter had been moving as well, an instant reflex had brought his Colt up and as the cobra struck Shelter's off-handed shot drilled the ugly head of the snake.

It slapped back against the wall, its head shattered, blood leaking down the boards. The roar of the .44 echoed in the wagon's confines and smoke curled through the room. Yet no one came running and Shelter was left to holster his Colt slowly, studying the deadly, lifeless cobra.

Picking up his saddlebags Shelter took his soap and towel. Walking out to the rain barrel he washed his chest, shoulders and arms, cooling his face with the water. Then he slowly put on his shirt and buttoned it.

McGinnis was at the long lunch table, cutting himself a bit of steak. He swirled it in the gravy on his plate and thrust it between his rubbery lips, chewing it with zeal.

There was a smile on his mouth as he chewed. Swede and Killanin noticed it and they smiled in return. It was Swede, leaning back to stretch who saw the tall man first, and his chair slapped forward. Yet he could not bring himself to speak, to move.

McGinnis noticed the odd look on Swede's face. "What the hell's the matter?" he asked around a mouthful of meat.

Before Swede could reply, McGinnis got the answer.

Shelter Morgan was behind him and he threw it on McGinnis' plate. McGinnis jerked away from the table, his face going flat white. The dead cobra lay across his plate, dripping blood. McGinnis spun around in a rage, but Shelter had his Colt out, the cold barrel pressed against McGinnis' neck.

"Eat it," Shell said. His eyes were utterly hard, his jaw set. When he spoke again, between his teeth, McGinnis could read the cold intent in the tall man's voice.

"I said, eat it!"

"You've got to be . . . " Shell's pistol lifted and he slammed it down, cracking McGinnis' skull. Blood ran from the big man's dirty hair.

"It's good and fresh," Shelter told him loud enough for everyone at the table to hear. "I just shot it—in my bed." Then he drew back the hammer on that pistol. "I told you to eat it, McGinnis."

McGinnis shakily picked up his knife and fork, feeling the muzzle of that Colt against his neck. He managed to cut a chunk of meat off the cobra, but as he lifted it toward his lips, a wave of nausea swept over him, and he felt his guts tighten and turn.

"I can't . . . " Sweat beaded on his forehead. "Damn it—the thing is poisonous. It could make a man sick!"

"Not near as sick as getting bit," Shelter said.

He nudged McGinnis with his pistol and the roustabout gave it another try, lifting that raw cobra meat to his lips.

"Damn you, Jones!" he muttered. "Damn you to a bleeding hell! You gun hawks are all the same. Give you bastards a gun and you think you're something . . . "

McGinnis' jaw dropped and then his eyes brightened. Shelter had taken a step back

79

and now as McGinnis watched, he holstered his pistol.

"I don't need it for something like you," Shell said coldly. "I've been shovelling up better than you all morning, McGinnis."

Enraged, McGinnis came to his feet and in a lunging dive he went at Shelter, his thick fists clenched. He hooked a right at Shelter's head, but Shell ducked under and he shot a straight left into McGinnis' face, splitting his nose. Blood spewed from the roustabout's nose and he screamed in anger, striking out with wild lefts and rights.

Shelter side-stepped one, felt another graze his temple and a third catch his jaw hard enough to rock him. But he stepped back, giving himself a moment to clear his head.

McGinnis was grinning grimly, blood spattering his shirt, but he was too anxious. Shell jabbed him with two lefts, rocking McGinnis' head back; then the tall man hooked a crisp right to McGinnis' jaw and the circus man's head snapped around.

McGinnis' eyes were glazed, and he was having trouble breathing through that nose, but he was far from done. He feinted left and then charged at Shelter, knocking him into the table behind him.

The table tipped over, dishes and food scattering across the floor as the onlookers stepped back, some urging McGinnis on savagely.

They hit the floor together and McGinnis was on top of Shell, his knees on Shelter's shoulders. The big man slammed a right into Shelter's face and he raised it again, grim triumph on his doughy features.

But Shell's legs came up and his boots locked under McGinnis' chin. Then Shelter kicked out, hard, and McGinnis tumbled over backward, clutching at Shell's ankles.

Both men came to their feet. Shelter was just a second quicker, however, and as McGinnis came fully erect he pounded a fist against the roustabout's ribs, and there was a cracking of bone as the breath rushed out of McGinnis' lungs.

Now McGinnis backed off a step, warily. But Shelter followed him, throwing a chair out of his way as he stalked the big man.

McGinnis kicked out, trying for Shelter's groin, but Shell had seen that coming and he blocked it with a knee, answering with his own kick to McGinnis' kneecap.

McGinnis roared with pain and frustration — that kneecap was surely broken. He drove himself at Shell, but he was slower now and Shell side stepped him, tripping McGinnis.

He hovered over McGinnis as the man got unsteadily to his feet and then Shelter closed up shop.

He slammed a right into McGinnis' chin over the circus man's ineffective guard, and he saw McGinnis' legs buckle. Now Shelter swarmed over McGinnis, hammering him with pulverizing blows which snapped his head back and bloodied his battered face.

Shelter dropped his head beneath his shoulder and burrowed in, punching and bulling McGinnis backward. The big man held his hands up still, but they were open, useless in warding off the triphammer blows of Shelter Morgan's fists.

McGinnis slammed against the wall and Shelter was all over him, digging lefts and rights into his damaged ribs, smashing his lips to bloody pulp. Then he let go of a big one, a stunning right with all of his weight behind it, with the leverage of his legs and shoulders in perfect unison. McGinnis' eyes rolled back and he sagged to the floor, his lights out, his face and shirt front streaked with blood.

Shelter stood there a moment, his shirt in rags, his breath coming roughly. Then he turned and walked to the overturned lunch table.

Shelter picked up his hat and looked at the others who stood around them in a silent circle. Then he walked to the door, picking up the cobra first to drop it onto McGinnis' lap.

Outside the sun was bright, glaring against Shell's eyes. He staggered to the rain barrel and ran water over his head and neck.

McGinnis was a big man and he had tagged Shelter with a few good shots. Shelter fingered an egg-sized lump on his skull and winced at the pain that caused.

Shaking his head and wiping back his hair, Shell planted his hat and walked on across the yard to Hope's wagon. He tapped on the door and waited a minute.

82

Finally the door swung open and she stood there, beautiful in that white silk wrapper, her flaming hair across her shoulders.

"I wondered if you would show up . . . God! Mister Jones—what happened? No, come in and tell me."

Shell went up the three steps and into the wagon which was decorated with old posters, newspaper clippings and tintypes of the circus performers gathered before some building or other.

"Sit down. I'll get something to clean you up," Hope said. Shell found a red leather chair and he perched there, his hat on his knee while Hope bustled about getting a pan, a cloth and a green bottle of something or other.

"What in the world happened?"

"Just a little run-in with McGinnis," Shell shrugged. Hope leaned forward, touching the mint smelling medicine to the cut on Shelter's head. It stung some, but he hardly noticed it. Hope's perfume filled his nostrils, and as she leaned against him, dabbing at his wounds, her full breasts, unrestrained beneath that flimsy wrapper pressed against him.

"Tell me about it," Hope asked.

"All right." Slowly then Shelter told her about the cobra, the fight in the lunch room. She listened attentively, biting her lip once in displeasure.

"That sounds like some of Ed's work, putting them up to it."

"I thought it might be, too," Shelter agreed.

Hope sat on the settee opposite Shelter's chair and she asked him, "Why don't you just ride on out, Jones? Ed won't give up. It can only mean more trouble for you."

"I can't," Shell said quietly.

"Why?"

"There's a lot I haven't learned about the circus that I'd like to—about circus folks." He smiled and she returned his smile.

Hope rinsed out the cloth she hed once again and dabbed at the cut on Shelter's head. She leaned down then and said softly into his ear, "You'd better take off your shirt. Let me tend to you."

Shell stood and peeled off his shirt. There was an abrasion low on his back where he had crashed into the table and Hope dabbed at that with her liniment.

"Does that make it feel any better?" she asked, standing in front of him.

"A little. Is that the best medicine you've got?"

"No." Hope undid her wrapper which was tied at the waist and she leaned forward, her breasts against Shelter's bare chest, her lips parted as she turned her mouth up to his.

Shelter took her in his arms, tasting her lower lip, brushing her upper lip before opening his mouth to her full kiss which was warm, wet, eager.

"Just a minute," she said breathlessly, and she crossed the room to lock the door. When she turned from that her robe had fallen open and Shelter had a tantalizing view of her white, pink nippled breasts, those tapering white legs, the lush red patch of hair between those thighs.

Shelter felt a stirring in his crotch and as Hope threw her robe aside, it became a throbbing insistence. He was straining against the jeans he wore and Hope noticed it.

She crossed the room and went to her knees, slowly unbuckling his belt, working at the buttons on his jeans. Her fingers trembled as she worked on Shell's fly, but finally she got the job done and Shelter's erection came free before Hope's delighted eyes.

Hope's hands went to his cock and she touched it with wonder, feeling the blood pounding through its length. Shell touched her hair, her ears as she explored him, her fingers administering loving touches; he watched her heft his balls, her eyes lighted.

Then he sat, kicked off his boots and jeans and stood again, naked, ready. Hope had scooted across the floor and she lay now against a tiger skin, her profuse red hair spread against the black striped background, and Shelter went to her.

She lifted her arms to him and Shell fell into them, tasting her lips, her throat with his mouth. Her hands went to his shaft, and she toyed with it, inflaming Shell's passion as he kissed her breasts, his tongue running in circles around her taut nipples.

They clung together and Shell's hand slipped between Hope's thigh, touching her moist sanctuary as she increased her stroking of his cock, tugging him toward her, her breathing increasing to a demanding series of gasps. Her legs spread more widely as Shell's fingers explored her soft, inner flesh and her mouth sucked at his, not wishing to wait a moment longer.

"Jones . . . !" Hope's knees came apart still more and she drew him toward her, her hands running across his solid buttocks, his massive cock, those hard-muscled thighs.

Shelter followed her, knowing that she was impatient for him now and he nestled between her legs, letting her take his erection, touch it to her softness, let it hover at the warm, honeyed entrance to her womb. Then she clawed at him, drawing him into her, gasping at each inch gained, her hands kneading his buttocks, her legs going farther apart until she could spread them no more, and then up as she thrust herself against Shelter Morgan, taking him in until he hit bottom and she cried out.

"God! You'll split me. It's going through. More!" she panted and Shell rolled against her, his hands finding her firm white ass, holding her higher yet as he drove it home, sending shock waves of pleasure through every fiber of Hope who shook, trembled, grabbed at him, wanting it all, getting it as they swayed together, Hope's juices rolling from her, trickling down her thighs, filling their nostrils with her womanly scent.

She lifted her head, bit at Shell's chest and

watched, with deep animal satisfaction as Shell's huge erection penetrated her, parting her soft reddish bush, sliding in and out between her smooth thighs with the juices of her body glossing its thick whiteness.

"Jones..." She clung to his shoulders, her head rolling from side to side, her pelvis slamming against Shell's, her body trembling, flashing with heat and liquid release as she watched his face, touched his working erection, felt her muscles tighten and then go slack, a gushing release causing her to go faint as brilliant colors and patterns flashed in her mind, as she worked against the hard muscled man, touched him, touched herself, felt his stroking build to an intense, driving rhythm which drove every sensation but one from her body, her mind.

She was swaying, her eyes rolled back, those magnificent legs locked around Shelter's waist. As he filled her with his cock he watched her fingers grabbing at him, and he felt himself tighten, felt himself begin to come. He lifted her higher and shoved it deep, feeling the fluids of her body smeared against him, feeling her clutch at him, her lips and hands touching wherever they reached as her demand rose again.

Hope tensed, spread her legs and caressed his buttocks feeling him go tight, feeling him drive it home again and again, and then, poised over her, fill her with his own hotly flowing orgasm, and she came again, trembling to exhaustion and she lay back, utterly limp, utterly still but for her fingers which drummed against his still twitching buttocks.

"Oh . . . Mister Jones," she murmured and then her eyes closed and she let relaxation conquer her as desire ebbed. And she lay still, utterly content, utterly satisfied.

They lay on that tiger skin quietly for long minutes, the only movement Hope's fingers tracing patterns on Shell's back. And then there was a tap at the door. Shelter moved.

"Don't move," Hope begged.

"One of us better answer that door," Shell told her. He stroked her hair and kissed her lightly, and she nodded as the rapping came again, more insistently.

Hope picked her wrapper up from the floor and Shelter watched as she moved to the door, her long legs flashing beneath the light fabric.

"Oh, it's you, Ed," he heard her say.

"We had some trouble—I need to talk to you."

"It'll have to wait," Hope answered. "What is it?"

"It's about that new man. He's got to go, Hope," Ed said passionately.

"We'll talk later—I'm not dressed," Hope responded. "Besides, I already heard the story. It doesn't sound like Jones is the one who's stirring up all the trouble to me."

"You've already heard . . . ?"

"Ed," Hope interrupted, and her voice was brittle. "I said later. I'm not dressed, and I'm not feeling well."

There was a long silence before Ed answered, "All right," and Shelter knew something was going through the circus manager's mind. Perhaps he sensed it, or maybe it was only Hope's remark that she had already heard the story, but Ed was not happy as he said "good-bye."

Slowly Hope closed the door, carefully locking it again. Then she turned, fluffing up her red hair in a nervous gesture. Shelter still lay on the tiger skin, and her eyes brightened as she studied his long, lean body, his equipment.

She walked to the tiger skin rug and sat beside Shelter, still wearing her robe and that hungry expression.

"Who are you anyway?" she asked Shelter.

"A drifter," he shrugged.

"That's all?"

"A good friend," Shelter grinned.

"Yes." She smiled and leaned forward, kissing his chest, letting a finger linger to play with the dark hair there. "But you're not a friend of Roland Blue?" she asked, lifting an eyebrow.

"No. You couldn't say that."

"I'm glad of that." Her hand rested on Shell's shoulder, and now she withdrew it, her green eyes thoughtful, distant.

"How about you, Hope?" Shell asked.

"What do you mean?"

"Just who are you? You don't seem to be a performer. And I've seen the way Ed acquiesces to your wishes, consults with you."

"Oh, that." She waved a hand. "That's just habit, I suppose. You see, Jones—God I wish you had chosen another name . . . "

Shell smiled, faintly, and Hope went on.

"This is my circus. Was . . . that's hard to accept. It *was* my circus, but we never really made much. Then we had a fire and there was nothing left but the animals and a group of performers who hadn't been paid for a long while.

"Roland Blue showed up suddenly, and he wanted to buy it. What else was there to do —I sold it to him, and he allows me to stay on as a sort of manager. He knows nothing about the circus, really. He doesn't seem to care much either. He doesn't even seem to care if we turn a profit."

"The way he schedules your performances, I can't see how there could be any profit," Shelter commented.

Hope looked at him curiously, and Shell felt compelled to add:

"Some of the boys were complaining about traveling from Kansas City to New Orleans to Houston with nary a stop in between."

"It's true," Hope admitted, "and it's hard to fathom just what Roland Blue has in mind. I've given up asking. He won't tell me what his plans are."

"You don't mind living like this?" Shelter asked.

"On the move?" Hope laughed. "My parents

were circus people in Europe. I was born in a wagon like this outside of Prague. I never remember spending more than a week in the same town. And then, circus people have always been my only friends. The townspeople have a mistrust of us. They treated us like gypsies, sure that we were out to rob them and then hit the road . . . Mind it? It's the only life I've ever known. What else could I do?

"But," she added soberly, "I do miss knowing this is mine—seeing to the details, even the worrying. That, I miss. I feel just a little useless, and that's a feeling no one likes."

"You're not hardly useless," Shelter said with a smile, and he drew her down to him.

"I was thinking," Hope said as Shelter's lips found her breasts, her throat. "With what happened today—why, it's not safe for you to sleep in the roustabout's wagon tonight."

"Funny," Shelter answered, "I was thinking the same thing."

Hope laughed and she opened her robe to Shelter's searching lips. He paused and she looked down at him with curiosity.

"What is it?"

"I was just wondering—that fire you had, Hope. Was there anything suspicious about it?"

"Was it set . . . I don't know. Why?"

"Just wondering. It's kind of curious, isn't it? A fire burns you out and suddenly a man shows up to bail you out. Only this man's not a circus man, as you say he seems to have little interest in it. But he buys it all the same. It gives a man reason to wonder."

"It does. But we don't need to wonder about it now, do we?" She fell against him, her lips searching his body, and Shelter had to agree.

"No. Not just now." And he wrapped her in his arms.

7.

The knocking at the door awakened Shelter and he sat bolt upright, his hand going to the Colt which rested on the chair beside the bed. Hope sat up sleepily, her breasts falling free of the sheet while she peered through her mass of red hair toward the door, yawning.

"What time is it?" she wondered.

It was early, that was certain. No light seeped through the curtains hung across the high window of Hope's wagon. She slipped from the bed and wrapped her gown around her, wiping back her hair as Shelter watched.

Hope walked through the dark wagon to the door. "Who is it?" she asked, and after a moment there was an answer.

"Ed. Sorry to awake you, Hope, but it's important."

Motioning for Shelter to be silent, Hope slipped out the door and he could hear them speaking in low voices, although he could not make out the words.

After a minute she re-entered the wagon and Shelter, who was sitting sleepily on the edge of the bed, looked up quizzically.

"What is it?" he wanted to know.

"We're moving out," she told him, her tone unaccepting. "Ed got a message from Mister Blue. He wants us to be rolling this morning."

"So soon?" Shelter frowned. "Where to now?"

"Mexico," Hope said, her voice filled with puzzlement.

"Mexico," Shell repeated.

"Some sort of private performance for the nobility . . . I didn't get it all. There was one other thing."

"Yes?"

"Ed wants you to report to him. Somehow he guessed you were here."

"All right," Shell agreed. "What was his mood?"

"Worried, I think. He sounded as if he really wants to talk to you. I don't think it's any sort of a trick—Ed knows I wouldn't stand for seeing you hurt."

"I'll see what he does want," Shell said, slipping into his jeans, stomping on his boots.

"You be careful." Hope came to him and stood on tiptoes, kissing him deeply, her hands gripping his shoulders.

"I will. But I thought you were sure he wouldn't try anything."

"With Ed? I don't think he will, but with Ed you're never really sure of anything. You just watch yourself."

"I mean to," Shelter told her.

She watched from the door as he crossed the circus yard. No hint of sunrise yet brightened the eastern horizon, and the yard was dark, with only the faint illumination of the dying moon behind the oaks.

The lamp was on in Ed's wagon and Shelter went on up, knocking on the door. At Ed's summons he entered. The big man was alone in the wagon and he waved a hand at a chair.

"I didn't know if you'd come or not, Jones," Ed said. "I didn't know if you trusted me enough to do it."

"Should I?" Shelter asked.

"No." Ed chuckled. A mirthless little laugh, it twisted his rubbery face into a cartoon of itself. "I guess you shouldn't trust me. But then," he added soberly, "I guess you don't. But that doesn't matter just now."

"No?"

Ed tapped his stubby fingers on his desk

top and studied the tall, cool man opposite him for a moment, meeting those blue-gray eyes with his own watery gaze.

"Tell me one thing, Jones; are you working for this circus or not?"

"I am," Shelter nodded.

"All right. Then it's time for you to start earning your pay." Ed snagged two white ceramic cups from the shelf behind him and poured coffee from the fresh pot he had on his desk.

"What have you got in mind?" Shelter asked.

"We're rolling out this morning—I don't know if anybody told you."

"I heard a rumor."

"You hear where we're going?" Ed asked, sipping his coffee. He made a face as he tasted it. "I am going to get a cook who knows how to make coffee one day."

"I heard tell we might be going into Mexico— long damned way."

"With scarce trails. I've been told the Comanches are active everywhere west of Houston."

"I've heard the same," Shelter answered, sipping his own coffee which was dark, strong, bitter.

"This is the way I read you, Jones, correct me if I'm wrong. I've seen the way your saddle is rigged, the boots you wear—them high-heeled jobs. I've seen the rifle you carry and the way you let that Colt revolver ride your hip. You're no greenhorn. I'd say you've ridden the West, I'd say you've seen a deal of it."

"A deal," Shelter nodded. Arizona, Mexico, California. He had seen some of Texas and Colorado. New Mexico and Wyoming in summer drought and winter snow. "I've seen a deal of this country."

"Indians?"

"I've known some, fought some." And loved one, he could have added, but did not. What was Ed getting at?

The big man threw his elbows up on the desk and got to the point. "This is as far west as I've ever been, Jones. I haven't got a man on this crew who has seen Texas before, let alone crossed it. They're roustabouts, circus men, not gunfighters, cowhands or plainsmen. Not that they're not fighters—you should know that—but they don't know how to find water, how to read Indian sign, nor shoot much. You do."

"That's right," Shell answered. "Not that I'd rank myself with the top scouts, but I've seen some trails. It might be you'd want to find someone who knows Texas well, who knows the Comanche—frankly, I don't."

"Damnit, Jones, I would if I could! If for no other reason than that we haven't gotten along. But we're dropping that big tent at sunrise, and we're rolling. I want you to lead us into Mexico." He read the uncertainty on Shell's face. "Unless you're ready to pull out now."

"No, I'm not ready. I'm sticking. And I guess I'd rather be scouting than cleaning up after your elephants."

"You'll do it then?"

"Like you said, I'm working for the circus. I'll do what you want me to. But," he warned Ed, "you're begging for trouble, you truly are. A slow moving train of circus wagons, heading where water is scarce and Comanche plentiful, with women, greeners, and few weapons—it's a damned boondoggle, Ed. No matter who scouted for you, you'd be lucky to get through to Mexico."

"I know it," Ed replied, and his voice revealed the uneasiness he felt. "But that's all there is to do unless I want to pull out, leave the circus, and I don't. My boss wants us rolling toward Mexico, and what Mister Blue wants, he gets."

"I'll get my roll together," Shelter said, rising from the chair. He put his empty coffee cup on Ed's desk, and Ed studied the tall man more closely. Maybe he had underestimated this Mister Jones—the man was cool, ready.

"Any questions?" Ed wanted to know.

"When's payday?" Shelter asked wryly.

"End of the trail."

"That's smart." Shell nodded and tugged his hat down. "Make sure all the water barrels you can find are filled, all right?"

"All right," Ed agreed, rising from his desk. "Anything else?"

"There's not much else we can do, is there?" Shelter asked. Then he turned and walked down the three steps to the wagon, watching the red line of sunrise crease the eastern skies as the circus came to life.

The men were grumbling. It was early and there had been no breakfast before setting to work. Tent stakes were pulled up, the elephants helping, bleachers pulled down and wagons hastily packed as the sun rose higher and tempers wore short.

Shelter took no hand in the work. Watching the operation from horseback, he met a few cold stares. McGinnis, of course, was still smarting from the beating he had taken, and Danny, his arm splinted and bound, watched Shelter sullenly from the steps of the roustabout's wagon. The others from that crowd shared the mood.

"Got nothin' to do?" Swede asked.

"Plenty," Shelter answered flatly. "But that's not my job any longer."

"No? You been promoted pretty fast."

"I wouldn't call it a promotion," Shell replied, "but I'll be takin' charge when we're moving. If you or any of the others can't take orders from me, you'd best drop out right now."

"Take orders . . ." Swede sputtered. "I'll be damned!"

"That's the way it's going to be," Ed said. He had come up beside Shelter, catching the tail end of the conversation. "You don't have to like it, Swede, hell—I don't like it. But that's the way it is, and like Jones told you, if you can't do it, draw your pay."

Swede swallowed a curse and walked away. They could see him muttering to McGinnis who turned dark, angry eyes on them as the two men coiled some heavy line.

"Thanks, Ed," Shelter said.

"Don't thank me. I didn't do it for you. It's for the good of the circus. I just want everyone to know how things stand. Just don't get the idea that they're going to swallow it meekly. You're new, you're unpopular as a skunk. They don't like you being in charge."

"I'll tread lightly where I can," Shell answered.

"Do that."

Ed swaggered away, and Shelter watched him go. McGinnis and Swede both straightened up from their work as Ed came to them.

"Did you mean that?" McGinnis demanded. "About Jones being in charge."

"I did."

"Hell of a fast promotion, wasn't it? But I guess he's been pulling strings, from what I hear."

"What do you hear, McGinnis?" Ed wanted to know, and his broad face was set, hard.

"I hear that Jones don't worry about his pay. Not with the fringe benefits he's pulling down. Miss Hope . . ."

"Shut your damned face!" Ed exploded.

"Hell, it's the damned truth, ain't it?"

"I said shut your mouth." Ed took a step forward and McGinnis backed away a little.

He had already taken one beating, and he had seen Ed work before. He was a rough bull when he was riled. "I won't hear any man on this crew talk about Hope."

"That shows you where we stand, Swede," McGinnis spat. "We can't even talk about her. The new man gets to screw her."

Ed boiled over at that and he stepped in, his big fist smashing against McGinnis' face, splitting his ear, slamming the roustabout to the ground where he lay across the coil of rope, unmoving.

"Get up, you son of a bitch!" Ed growled, but McGinnis did not move. "Get the hell out of here, then. Pick up your pay and blow. No sense you hanging around either, Swede," Ed added as an afterthought.

Then he spun and stamped away, his big fists still clenched. McGinnis got slowly to his feet, touching his ear which still trickled blood.

"That's two of them now, Swede," he said blackly. "Two men I got to square accounts with."

It was noon before they were packed up, and they rolled out beneath the glaring Texas sun, leaving three men behind: Danny, Swede, and McGinnis. Maybe, Shelter thought, they were the lucky ones.

Ahead lay the long, sun blistered plains, waterless stretches where only the coyote, the rattlesnake and the Comanche seemed able to survive.

The Apache were consummate soldiers, but they were men who preferred to fight on foot. The Comanche were cavalry—the fiercest the world has ever seen. Shelter had heard the stories, and he had no confidence in the ability of his band to either elude or outfight skilled Comanche warriors.

The enemy would be quicker, better equipped for warfare, more sure of the terrain. He turned slightly in the saddle, watching the wagons line out behind him, slow heavy wagons carrying wild animals and trapeze lines when they should have been loaded with food, water, guns.

But Shelter was into it now, and there was no turning back. Somewhere ahead was Roland Blue; somewhere the Comanche. Shelter pulled his hat lower against the ball of the sun and heeled the big black forward.

They followed the coast for the first few days, trying to avoid the Indians in that way. The hurricane which everyone had prophesied seemed to have dissipated or moved out to sea once more, for they had clear weather along the Gulf, but the sand grew deeper and travelling difficult.

Twice they spent half the day digging out of deep dunes, and without the elephants they never would have made it at all.

"We're going to have to move inland," Shelter told Ed.

"I know it." Sweat rained from the fat man's

face as the two men watched the colorful wagon train work through yet another mile of dunes. The ocean roared against the beach, and the air was fresh, salt scented. A mile or so inland it would grow sultry, hot.

"The last good water I know of is the Colorado," Shell went on. "From there it's going to be tough, really tough."

"We've got no choice," Ed shrugged.

The town he wanted to hit was south and west, east of Nuevo Laredo, a place called Tortuga. Shelter had never heard of it, but there was much he did not know about Mexico.

"These upper-crust folks," he asked Ed, "how is it they live in a place like Tortuga? It can't be much of a town."

Ed shrugged again. "I suppose they've got them a rancho there. I couldn't say."

The two men walked through the dunes, Shelter leading the black, watching the low blue line of Padre Island to the south. "These folks—you said they were nobility or some such? Just what does that mean? I thought they had a republic in Mexico now."

"I couldn't say. Blue knows . . . you're damned curious, aren't you, Jones?"

"Yes, sir, I am." Shelter stopped and faced the big man. "We're riding through hell and hell's armies to get to Tortuga. My life's riding on this, the same as yours. I just like to know what I'm risking my neck for."

"I couldn't tell you much more than I have." Ed looked off toward the sea again, wiping his

103

broad, white forehead with his scarf. "I'm ridin' blind too."

"Why? Why are you riding blind, Ed?"

"Because it's my job, damnit. Just like it's yours, Jones. I told you how it was back in Houston. If you're working for the circus, you do like Mister Blue says. That's all there is to it."

"It just seems we're risking a hell of a lot," Shelter commented. He nodded back toward the wagon train where Hope stood, hands on hips, watching them, her flaming red hair tousled by the sea breeze. "Hope too."

Ed was silent for a long moment. He started to say something else, but changed his mind. Instead he walked back toward the wagon train, climbing up in the box of Hope's yellow wagon beside her.

Shell stepped into leather and turned westward, away from the coast, away from the coolness, toward the dry desert beyond, toward the Comanche stronghold.

The days began to drag. Endless yellow plains crossed only by the broken trail they followed, a trail which seemed to lead nowhere. Here and there were scattered cholla cactus or greasewood, but aside from this dry, thorny vegetation, the land was barren.

Yellow dust curled up from under the wagons' wheels, smothering all of them. The animals grew restless, hot and sick of the constant motion. From time to time one of the big cats roared out its rage.

Shelter rode ahead of the train, squinting against the devil sun, trying to pick up first sign of water . . . or of Comanches.

At night he slept apart from the camp, where the night was still and he could hear better, where the firelight did not dull his night vision.

Not that he did not hunger for that red-haired woman but the wagon was the last place he wished to be caught if and when there was trouble.

The nights were cold. Brittle stars hung in a black velvet sky, and dawning brought instant heat. Shelter swung into camp for breakfast which was most often nothing but coffee and sourdough.

The man named Killanin was hunkered over his coffee cup and he looked up at Shelter out of red-rimmed eyes.

"How's things out there?"

"Quiet."

Killanin nodded and sipped at his coffee. "Jones, let me ask you this. Do you know where in hell you're leading us?"

"I've a notion," Shelter said.

"That's all?"

"I'm afraid that's all," Shell admitted.

The roustabout nodded, understanding slowly seeping in. "You don't know where the water is out here. Even if there is any."

"That's right, Killanin."

"Damn," the circus man breathed. He looked down the long backtrail as if wishing could take him back to Houston, then, tossing his coffee dregs to hiss against the fire, he rose and walked back toward his wagon.

Shelter finished his own coffee and then got up, stretching his arms. The night had been cold and he still had a stiffness in his joints.

Then he saw a sight to warm him and he smiled, walking through the breakfasting performers and roustabouts to where Hope waited, a smile on her beaming face.

"Back here," she beckoned, and he stepped around to the side of the wagon where she waited, leaning against it. Shelter leaned against her, his hand on the wagon, and his lips met hers.

"God I've missed you," Hope said. She let her finger run down his brown throat to the V of his open shirt.

"I'll make it up to you," Shelter promised.

"I believe you will," Hope answered, her lips meeting his in a dozen short, questing kisses.

Shell drew her into his arms and he could feel her heart pounding. Hungrily he searched her mouth, felt her respond.

"Jones!" Ed's voice boomed and Shelter turned to see the big man standing there, a rifle in his hands. "Untangle yourself—we've got riders coming in from the north."

8.

Shell snatched up his Winchester and walked with Ed to the northern approach. There were others gathered there already; a tattooed man; Ben Tillits who threw knives at his wife; and Tramp Garber, the little elephant handler.

Shelter shouldered his way through the crowd, Ed beside him. There were riders coming in all right. A dozen or so. Men in blue, they were—or had been. The dust and alkali had bleached their uniforms white, frosted their ponies and their hair.

As they drew nearer Shell could read the pained weariness etched on their faces, and he could see that they were not totally sound. Several had bandages on, stained with maroon. One trooper wore a bandage across his face, with only his nose showing; another had both arms in slings.

Their leader was a slender, hawk faced captain. He rode up to where Morgan and Ed waited and he sat his weary horse, surveying the circus wagons.

"Who's the damned fool leading this outfit?" the captain asked.

"Me." Ed stepped forward and the captain shook his head. Some of his men had slipped from their horses and they led them forward to the wagon train.

"No water!" Shelter called over his shoulder and the soldiers pulled up short, their angry eyes switching to Shelter Morgan. "Sorry," Shell told the captain, "but it's all we got, and I don't know when we'll find more."

"If you're heading west, you won't find any more ever," the cavalry officer shot back. "All right . . . can you let my men have a swallow if we hold the horses back?"

"Yes." Shelter nodded, again studying the wounded soldiers. "Had a rough time of it?"

"You'd better damned well believe it." The captain stepped down from his weary, salt flecked roan as Tramp Garber brought

108

a couple of water sacks out for the parched soldiers. A big shouldered sergeant came up to stand beside the officer. He took a drink from Garber's bag, nodded thanks and wiped his forehead.

"We lost sixteen men," the sergeant volunteered.

"It's Iron Heart," the captain went on. He too took a quick swig of water. "That's one mean Comanch' — and one tough one. But you folks, haven't you heard of this trouble? You can't go out there." He glanced back toward the empty plains and shuddered a little as if glad he had made it back, and aware of how small a margin they had survived the desert by.

"We're going on," Ed said with determination.

"Then you're a damned fool." The captain said it without malice, but with wonder. "I see you've got women, too. Just what the hell is going through your mind, circus man?"

"We're simply following through on a contract. We're entertainers. We're going where the job is."

"Entertainers!" The sergeant laughed and replaced his hat. "Iron Heart will find you right entertaining, I'd say. Unfortunately, you won't find him to be much amusement."

"Sergeant Connors is right. More than right," the captain said. "Taking all these people out there — you're inviting a massacre, sir.

"Turn around, for God's sake," someone

shouted, and Shelter glanced over toward the muffled voice. It was the man whose face was swathed in bandages. The voice came from behind all that gauze, "Go back! Go back before it's too late!"

There was panic in the voice, hysteria. "Sergeant," the captain said in a low voice and the sergeant nodded, going to the injured trooper. "One of the Comanches was over him with a scalping knife when we found him," the officer said quietly. "The job was half done."

"God." Tramp Garber turned away, his stomach turning over.

"What do you think, Jones?" Ed asked.

"I think the man is right," Shelter replied.

"So do I. But I'm taking this circus through anyway."

"It'll be without me!" It was Tillits, the knife thrower. His wife was huddled against him. "Captain, can you escort my wife and me back to Houston?"

"You're welcome to ride with us," the officer agreed.

Ed was furious. "Tillits, you owe this circus. I've loaned you money, seen you were fed. You'll not find another circus to take you in if you pull out on me."

"No? Maybe I'm in the wrong line of work then. I'll maybe not find another show to hook on with, but I'll damn sure not find another life if the Comanche want my hair or doesn't that concern you?" Tillits waited for an answer, but there was none from Ed. "I'll turn my

110

wagon," the knife thrower said.

He was not alone. The Genoas, the trapeze artists, pulled out too, and the fat lady. Ed stood beside Shelter, watching the weary band of soldiers lead the circus wagons back toward the coast, toward safety.

"You, Jones," Ed said without looking at Shelter. "You could have turned back. Why didn't you? What the hell is so important to you about getting this circus to Mexico?"

"I signed on for the job."

"No." Ed's brown eyes slowly searched Shelter's eyes. "You might be stubborn, but not this stubborn. You've got other reasons."

"Do I?"

"You do. Maybe I don't want to know what they are, though. Not now—I need you too much right now."

"You know, Ed, I could ask you pretty much the same question. You can't be this stubborn either. You're risking your life to please your boss, to put on one lousy performance . . . that don't quite ring true. You want to tell me what your reasons are?"

"No. Let's let it lie for now, Jones. It'll come out in the end, I expect."

"I expect so," Shelter Morgan said, and there was an odd, humorless smile on his lips which Ed could not quite read. He nodded slowly, to himself, and then walked heavily off toward what remained of the circus caravan.

Hope was beside Shelter now and she too watched the departing wagons for a long while.

111

Finally Shelter asked her, "Why don't you go too, Hope? There's time to catch up. I'd hate to see you hurt."

"I won't leave you," she answered. "Nor will I leave my circus. It is still mine. Roland Blue might have the papers on it, the contracts, but it is mine, Jones. It was mine long before he came along, and it will be mine again when he's gone.

"I can't leave—it would be abandoning my home, my work, my life. Then what would be left for me?" Those emerald green eyes locked with Shelter's. "Not even you."

There was water at the Colorado, but little enough. The river ran shallow, thick with red silt. The banks were a good fifty feet apart at this point, but the river itself ran four to five feet wide. There was enough for the stock, and enough to fill their barrels. Yet Shelter was worried. If the Colorado was down to a trickle, then the San Antonio and the Nueces rivers likely were the same, or completely dry. *That* could prove fatal.

Not that they had enough water in those barrels to make it to the Nueces anyway. Somehow water must be found on the desert, and it was up to Morgan to find it. He discussed it with Ed.

"I'll ride out early and stay a day ahead, maybe two."

"And if you don't find water?" Ed asked.

"Well—I won't be back in that case. That'd be a bit of luck for you."

112

"Luck? What do you mean, Jones?"

"I mean Hope. A man can tell you've got a case on her, likely have had for years."

"You're crazy."

"Maybe, but not blind. Is she the reason you stick with this circus, Ed?"

"If it was, it wouldn't be intelligent of me, would it? She can't see me for sour apples. I wish I knew how you . . . " Ed shut up, shaking his head.

"Make sure you keep those wagons circled and a guard out, will you?" Shelter was watching as the elephants cooled themselves in the red river water. "Them Comanch' would likely as not slip right up on you anyway, but don't take a chance where you don't have to. My other advice would be to have two outriders set to sound the alarm."

"All right, if you think that's additional protection."

"Ed, there's not going to be any protection against Iron Heart's warriors, I thought you understood that. Listen, Ed. I might not come back from this excursion. If I don't, if you care about Hope, give a damn about your own skin and that of the others — give it up. Turn north and try to make it to Schulenburg or even San Antonio. Anyplace where there's folks gathered together, where there's water. Because," he added soberly, "you'll damned sure never make Mexico without water."

Ed made no response, but he knew Shelter was right. He watched as the tall man turned

113

then and walked to Hope's wagon.

Shelter knocked on the wagon door. She was inside and her eyes brightened as she opened the door.

"Mister Jones." She stood aside, but Shelter shook his head.

"I can't come in. I only came by to tell you I was riding out."

"But you'll be back?"

"I hope so," Shelter grinned. "I've got to find us some water, Hope. I've already told Ed, now I'd like to say it to you. If I'm not back in two days, turn these wagons north. There's no chance of making Mexico without more water. None at all. You do understand?" he asked, noticing the distant look in Hope's eyes.

"Yes, of course," she said quickly. "But I was thinking of the other part — if you aren't back — don't you expect to come back?"

"Right now I don't *expect* anything, Hope. If I'm able, I'll be back. You should know that." He stretched out his arms and took her into them, kissing her once before he turned and walked away, leading that black gelding through the yellow dust which swirled and drifted through the camp as the first wagons began to roll.

When Shelter looked back she was still there, watching from her wagon door, her red hair across her shoulders, looking small and helpless.

He stepped into leather and swung the black westward, not looking back again. It was a long, lonesome land, and a deadly one Shelter Morgan rode. Yellow hills and grassless plains. Black, basaltic rock, uncovered by time's winds, showed like glass along the ridges beneath the white hot sun.

There was the omnipresent cholla, some nopal cactus and red earth. No high mountains, no soft blues, no patches of shade broke the flatness of the land, the interminable distances which could have run to eternity.

Shelter slowed the black and turned in the saddle, seeing the circus wagons far behind, like matchboxes towed by black ants. He studied the landfall, guessing where water might be found, knowing that wherever water could be found, the Comanches were likely to be as well.

The afternoon sun dropped into Shelter's face and he tugged his hat low, watching the blindingly white distances. The land had grown more convoluted now, and he crossed a series of dry washes which were littered with water-rounded stones. But there was not a drop to be found now.

His own throat was parched, his tongue thick, but Shell held back on taking a drink. The horse could not and so he filled his hat and let the black have its water, keeping his eyes on the empty distances as he did so.

Sweat trickled down Shell's throat, and his shirt clung to him. The fragrant, dry scents of sage and dust mingled in his nostrils. He shaded his eyes and looked off to the north and then to the south. No one. Nothing.

Wearily he swung into the hot saddle, angling off across a dry lake bed. Dead, brown cattails lay pushed over around the perimeter of the cracked, dried lake bottom.

It was growing late now, the sun which hung in his eyes near the horizon growing red, streaking the pale sands with color. It was then that he saw it, quite suddenly, and unexpectedly.

To the south and west there was a patch of gray-green. It appeared only briefly and then was gone as Shelter dipped into a ravine. Urging the horse up the far side he turned that way. Grass, was it? Trees? He could not be certain, but he wanted to find it before it grew dark.

Already he had lost it to the shadows and the land. For although the land appeared flat here, it was broken at intervals by sudden, water washed gulleys, some hundreds of feet wide, all dry and deep in shadow at this hour.

Shelter stood in his stirrups, but could see nothing. And then he smelled it. Water, or damp foliage. The sun was only a reddish memory in the west and he zig-zagged his horse southward, startling a jackrabbit and then a stalking coyote.

And then he was there. How much water there would be, he could not tell. But there was a stand of sycamore low in an arroyo, some willow and rushes. A pond of water shone like a mirror through the sycamores, the late sun marking the end of the quest for Shelter Morgan.

"Let's have at it," Shelter told the horse,

"we've earned it."

They slid down a sandy bluff, the black going nearly to its haunches, and then approached the tree-screened pond cautiously. Shelter carried his rifle across the saddlebows. He had seen no tracks, had seen none all day, but this was no time to hurl caution to the winds.

He came slowly through the sycamores which were dark, deep in shadow but for the upper reaches where a thousand mirrors of light played. It was silent, still. Crickets sang in the undergrowth and a flight of dove winged across the pink, sundown skies.

Then Shelter came out on the sandy beach of the hidden pond and there was water. Sweet, crystal water.

And the lone Comanche.

9.

There was a purple twilight haze across the lake which still held one golden highlight. Ripples ran away from a small, feeding fish. The sycamores shaded the sandy beach. Leaning against one of those trees was a Comanche warrior, watching Shelter's approach out of black, hostile eyes.

He had no weapon which Shelter could see, nor did the Indian try to make a run for it, and coming nearer, the black's hoofs silent in the sand, Shelter saw why.

He was wounded, and badly. Scab clung to his chest and shoulder. His leg had been nicked as well. A purple and yellow bruise stained his stocky thigh. The leg might have been broken.

Shelter eased on toward him, his eyes flickering to the sycamore grove around him. There were no other Comanche, apparently. If there had been, Shelter figured he would be a dead man by now.

That didn't guarantee, however, that others would not be arriving, and Shelter kept his gun in hand as he stepped from the saddle, watching the tense, defiant face of the young Comanche brave.

Shelter walked to the pond and squatted down, tasting the water, his eyes on the brave. The black dipped its muzzle into the pond as well, and Shelter let it drink while he emptied out his canteen which was full of Colorado silt and filled it with this sweet, cool water which seemed to come from a spring.

The Comanche watched him, still wary, but perhaps more resigned. He could not fight; the white man would kill him. The brave's lips were cracked and blistered, his face was skinned from a fall he had taken somewhere.

A gourd dipper sat near his hand, but it was empty and the Indian watched thirstily as Shelter drank again from the pond. Shelter strode to him, his rifle in one hand, the canteen in the other.

"Water?"

The brave's black eyes glared at Shelter out of the twilight.

"Go ahead," Shelter urged him, "have yourself a drink."

The Indian did not move and Shelter dropped the canteen by his hand and went to unsaddle. He picketed the black back under the trees where there was a deal of gramma grass. When he walked back to where the wounded brave sat, carrying his saddlebags across his arm, he glanced at the canteen. If the brave had taken a drink, he had placed the canteen back down in the same exact spot, and Shelter would have bet the man had not touched the water.

"You'd better drink," Shelter said, nodding toward the canteen, but the brave did not move. "Well, do what you want then," Shelter told him. "Me — I'm hungry, and I mean to have something to eat."

He broke into his pack and took out some of Cooky's sourdough biscuits and some jerky. He chewed the salty, hard fare slowly, chasing it down with generous gulps of water.

There was a rising three-quarter moon and that provided enough light for Shelter to watch the brave by. The man's face was stoic, yet at moments when he thought Shelter was not looking, pain twisted his broad features.

"I'd give a lot for a cup of coffee. But I guess it's a bit risky to have a fire." He chewed on the biscuit and held one out to the brave. "Want one? They aren't bad. A mite stale, maybe, but not too bad." The Indian simply glowered at him, and Shelter shrugged.

He finished eating, watching the rising moon shine on the water. Then he put his gear away. Walking back to the Comanche he stood over him, his shadow falling across the man's face.

"You know you aren't going to make it. Not like that. Looks like you need a splint on that leg and a bandage on that chest wound."

The brave watched Shelter unblinkingly, his chest rising and falling.

"Without food or water . . . how long's it take you to drag yourself to that pond and back?" Shelter squatted on his heels and tipped his hat back. "I'd help you, partner, if you'd let me. But I'm much afraid you'd only think I was trying to finish you off. If you spoke . . . "

"I speak," the Comanche said quietly and Shelter grinned.

"So you do. Wish you'd of spoke up before. A man gets tired of talkin' to himself."

"You go away," the Comanche said. "Many braves come soon."

"Is that right?" Shelter looked around at the silent night. "They'd best come right soon, partner, or you won't be around to see it."

The Comanche clammed up and lifted his head proudly, but a wave of pain went through him and his face collapsed into a mask of discomfort.

"Let me see to them wounds," Shelter said quietly. "I'm no medicine man, but I reckon I can clean 'em up some, bind that leg."

121

"You are a crazy man! Don't you see me? Don't you know Comanche when you see Comanche!"

"I know what you are."

"I would kill you if I could!" the warrior said in exasperation.

"Yeah, I reckon you would. And, if I was to see that you meant to kill me out there, I'd fight back. But now we're not fighting. Now you're wounded, and I don't like to see a man lying wounded. Maybe I know how it feels."

"You are a crazy man. Many warriors will come here."

"Somehow," Shelter replied, "I'm not buying that. I think you're alone and I think you're going to die alone unless you let me help you."

"I don't want your help!"

"Partner, no man wants to die. Think of the hunts you still have ahead of you, the horses you will own, the squaws."

"Do what you like," the Comanche said as if it mattered not at all to him whether he lived or died.

Shelter washed his chest wound and bandaged it as well as possible with his shirt tail. The leg was a different story—it was a jagged, nasty wound with bone protruding through muscles.

"I'm going to have to pull that straight," Shelter told him. Sweat glistened on the brave's forehead, but he said nothing, only nodding to show that he understood. The warrior held tight to the tree trunk behind his back and Shelter got on the ankle, knowing it was going to hurt like hell, but that bone had to be set.

"Ready?"

The brave nodded again and Shelter took a deep breath, pulling and twisting on that shattered leg, the brave's face dripping sweat, his every muscle trembling spasmodically as Shelter yanked the ankle hard. But he did not cry out, would not allow himself to cry out.

Shelter eased the bone down and when he was satisfied that he had a match, he bound the leg as tight as possible using his spare blanket to pad it and straight branches cut from the sycamore tied with piggin strings. When he was through he sat back, wiping his own forehead, knowing he had caused the Comanche a tremendous amount of pain. He also knew that he had just possibly saved the leg.

The Comanche was shaking pretty bad now, probably shock had set in—nature saving him the full thrust of the pain.

Shell covered him with his blanket and went to the pond, filling the canteen again. The Comanche watched him out of glassy eyes as Shelter returned and set the water near to hand.

"Keep it, I've got a spare," Shelter said. "I'll leave you some of those biscuits as well."

The Comanche said nothing at all. To be prudent, in case the Indian had been telling the truth about others coming, Shelter decided to camp on the outcropping above the pond. It overlooked all of the surrounding territory, and with the horse to keep watch, he felt it would be a secure camp. He told the Indian as much, saddling as he talked.

"By the way," Shell added as he took the horse's reins, "they call me Shelter Morgan."

"Shelter Morgan," the Comanche repeated thickly. "Crazy Shelter Morgan."

Shell grinned and he got the merest of smiles in response. "Luck to you, boy," Shell said and then he led the black out, watching the moon shadows before him on the white sand.

The guns rang out and Shelter felt the breeze of a bullet whipping by within inches of his face. He slapped the black into a run, grabbing the saddlehorn at the same moment and they splashed into the pond at full tilt, shots filling the air with fire and lead. The pond was narrow and Shell hit the far side at a run, letting the black find its way through the sycamores. A few last, searching shots slammed into the tree trunks and then it was silent, dark and deadly.

Comanches? Somehow Shelter did not think so. Perhaps because he felt he would have been dead by now had it been Indians.

The moon was screened out by silver clouds, and the canyon was still. He stopped the black and listened. Afar off a horse nickered, and a second pony answered it. Shell put his hand on the black's muzzle to make sure it did not try to answer the others.

There was no advantage to being mounted,

but Shelter did not want to lose the black—not out here—and so he stayed in the saddle, his Colt limp in his right hand.

How many were out there? There was no telling, but there were at least two. By the flurry of the gunshots, he guessed three or four, possibly more.

He sat the black in the deep shadows, eyes searching the darkness. There was only one way out of that canyon that Shelter knew, and that was back in the direction of the hunters.

The minutes passed in slow progression. A cool breeze ruffled the leaves of the big sycamores, shuttling clouds before the pale face of the moon.

Slowly Shelter circled back toward the pond. He did not like the idea of moving, for to move was to make some noise. But he had to know what he was facing. If these were not Comanches, there was still a chance that the Comanches would be coming. Then there would be no escape.

Stealthily he crept through the trees, walking and leading the black, careful that he did not crush a twig underfoot, hoping the horse could somehow be as nimble.

He was behind a screen of trees now, among some big boulders and from there he could see down to the pond which was twenty or thirty feet below. The moon shimmered on the water and the trees swayed in the breeze, but nothing else moved.

The Comanche, Shelter realized suddenly,

was gone. In his condition it would have taken something for him to move himself. Perhaps his friends had come for him, although Shelter would have sworn the brave was lying, making up the tale to try to protect himself.

He lay unmoving for long minutes there in the darkness, listening for horses or a missed step. There was none.

Nothing. It was utterly silent.

Shelter slid back from between the boulders and they came at him. A white face loomed up out of the darkness and Shelter saw a gun come up. His was quicker, however and as the flame spewed from their muzzles the attacker screamed and was slammed back against a tree.

Beside Shell another man rushed out of the trees and Shelter side-stepped him, bringing his pistol down with deadly force, and he heard bone crack. He fired into the fallen man's body and had half-turned when he heard a shot from the trees, felt the sudden searing pain of a bullet biting his shoulder.

Shelter ducked behind the horse, angrily winged a shot at the trees and slid into a small, leaf filled depression, holding his fire, stilling his breath.

His arm was on fire and he could feel blood trickling down his sleeve, but Shelter did not move to attend to it. He stayed still, eyes fixed on the shadowy woods, waiting, knowing that the gunman was watching back, knowing that the first to move might be the first to die.

The moon shadows blended, separated and were blotted out as the minutes passed, as the clouds drifted by, silver against a black velvet sky.

Shelter heard an owl call from far away, he smelled the water below and he realized that his mouth was dry, cottony. He would have given a lot just then for that canteen which hung on his pommel. A lot, but not his life. He remained still, his muscles knotting. The black blew and looked around questioningly.

Shelter heard something. What, he was not sure. A boot crushing a leaf, perhaps, or brush scratching against someone's clothing. He looked in the direction the sound had come from, seeing nothing, his thumb locked over the hammer of that big blue Colt.

In the other direction a man moaned in pain, his voice breaking off into a sob. That was his tough luck—he had come looking for Shelter, meaning to kill him.

The sound came again. Then, as Shelter's eyes flickered back, he burst out of the bushes, firing with either hand and Shell fired back, rolling aside as the bullets dug furrows in the dark, leaf-littered earth around him.

The volley of shots roared against the night, and flame and the acrid scent of gunpowder filled the hollow. Then it was still.

The body of a man lay slumped against the earth, nearly at Shell's feet and Shelter stood, his head pounding, his body sticky with cold sweat.

With his foot he rolled the man over, face up to the fading moon.

It was McGinnis, and he was dead, three holes through his chest.

"You came a long ways to die, circus man," Shelter said. He stood over the man, his breath coming raggedly still, his arm throbbing painfully. From down the path the other man still moaned miserably.

Shelter ignored him. He sat on a rock and bound his arm up, using his teeth to get a knot. Then he went to where the wary black waited and took the canteen from the saddle horn. He took a deep drink and then washed his face, trying to shake off the numbness which had come with the bullet wound.

He tethered the black and then walked down the rabbit run, finding another dead man. It was Swede, and Shelter's bullet had taken him square in the middle of the forehead, killing him instantly.

Shelter picked up Swede's gun and tucked it behind his belt before walking the few steps to the wounded man who still moaned. Now that man looked up and his face went ashen as he saw Shelter Morgan standing over him.

"Hello, Danny. Got it again, did you?"

The kid was curled up against the ground, holding his wounded arm with his other which was still splinted from when Shell had broken it in Ed's office.

"I didn't want to come . . . McGinnis talked us into it." The kid's face was raining sweat.

He looked like hell. The bullet had nearly torn that arm off, it seemed like.

"You got to quit listening to folks," Shelter told him. He crouched down to look at the arm. It was a bloody, torn mess. "I don't think I can do much for that arm, Danny. But I'll try bandaging it. Maybe you can make it back."

"Hell, I'll never make it," the kid said. "You're right—I always listened to folks when they . . . wanted to take me along." Danny's voice wavered. He was sinking fast and he knew it.

"I'm sorry, kid, really," Shelter said.

"I know. I believe it. Hell, I was comin' at you. What else could you do? Same as before . . . you'd think a man would learn something once . . . before . . . I really don't want this, Jones! Damnit, I want to live!"

And then he was dead, and Shelter stood, knowing he could not have helped it. But he knew he had done it, and he never had liked that feeling no matter how badly the man had needed killing. Danny, he was just a wild kid riding with men who had less sense than he did. He never deserved it.

"Damn you, McGinnis," Shelter muttered to the night. Three men dead, and no reason for any of it but hurt pride. Shelter had seen many a man go under for the same reason—pride. It seemed easier for men to die than to swallow their pride, and that made no sense.

Shelter stripped Danny's cartridge belt off of the body, made sure they were .44-40s, and then he walked back to the black.

129

Stepping into the saddle he had to fight back the pain, but fight it back he did; then he wove his way through the trees, returning to the pond.

The Comanche was gone. Shelter called out and then combed the woods, but he did not find the brave.

Shelter again drank from the pond, washing his arm before binding it again. Then he refilled his canteens and stepped into leather again. The place, peaceful and beautiful as it was, had the stench of death about it now, and Shelter meant to ride south. Besides, if there was anyone else around out on that desert, the shots might call them there.

Shell rode out slowly. The night had closed out the pale moon and the black had to pick its way across rough, broken ground. There was no light to be seen anywhere but for a single star winking through a break in the clouds.

Despite the pain and the distances Shelter felt relieved. There was water, and plenty of it, for the circus train at the pond. They would only have to fill their barrels and get back out of that canyon trap before the Comanche did find them, and they would be provisioned well enough to make the Rio Grande and Mexico.

Then the danger would be behind them, and they could perform for their boss. Perhaps, Shelter thought with grim satisfaction, he himself would give a performance which

Roland Blue would never forget.

He rode through the night, buttoning his coat against the chill which came on in early morning, frosting the desert weirdly with a silver sheen.

By daylight he would meet the circus train and within two days they would reach the Rio Grande. He had missed Hope as well, and to tell the truth he was looking forward to a reunion with that red-haired woman, a close reunion.

His arm hung limply, shot through with pain at each jolt, with each misstep the black took, but they had made good time through the night, and he watched the rising red sun with welcoming eyes.

Yet the pleasure he derived from watching the warming sun rise and melt the frost of evening dimmed with each mile he rode.

It was not out there. Shelter guided the black to higher ground and stood in the stirrups, shielding his eyes with his hand. Nothing. The circus train which should have been nearly to him had vanished!

Shelter stepped down and walked, resting the horse which was already white with salt as the sun turned the earth beneath them to chalky dust.

Mile after mile he walked, his arm filled with hot pain, his scarf around his face to protect against the alkali dust. Nothing . . . the train which should have been visible for miles seemed to have been swallowed up by the sea of sand.

It was not until noon when the sun was a searing globe in the high, white sky that Shelter discovered the tracks. He pulled up short, smothering a bitter curse.

The wagon tracks led due south. Straight for Mexico, across a waterless desert, when their water barrels, he knew, were nearly dry. Ed hadn't listened. Why, Shelter did not know. But Ed had chosen to attack the desert, heedless of Shell's strong advice, heedless of the pain and death which could follow on the heels of such a decision.

There was just no way, no way at all for those people to survive. Maybe a few would, the strong, but for many others it would be a lingering death by dehydration.

What could make a man lead his people into the desert like that? There was no telling what had prompted Ed to make that decision, and Shelter knew only one thing.

They had elected to try it, and he would follow them. He had his own trails to travel, to end. The bloody end to one of those trails lay before the circus wagons, and so Shelter swung the weary black southward, following the deep ruts of the circus train which led across the trackless, arid wasteland.

10.

The day inched by, the only sound the scraping of the black's hoofs, the only reality on all the broad desert the searing sun, and the pain which tore at Shelter's shoulder.

Far off to the north a low, shadowed mesa rose off the floor of the desert, and to the south distant clouds bunched along the horizon. But for Shelter there was no shade, no screening clouds. Only the glare of the sun against the white earth, the rocky, cactus studded earth.

By sunset the black was a shambling, exhausted animal and Shelter was no better off. Their camp was only a patch of desert like any other patch of it. Shell tied the reins to the black to a flat rock and managed to get the saddle off. He sat on the raw earth, watching the sun fade to a deep crimson, knowing that he would have to ride nights or die beneath the sun.

"Sorry," he murmured to the black which pricked its ears up and nuzzled Shelter's shoulder. "It's been a long dry trail, and the end appears to be far off."

That horse was Wyoming born, and this desolate country was a far cry from its high country grasslands. Yet it was doing well enough considering the circumstances.

Shell washed his arm which was blotched purple, but appeared clean where McGinnis' bullet had taken him. Then, as purple dusk settled, he drank sparingly from his canteen and ate the last two biscuits which were now hard as rocks, salty, tasteless.

He allowed himself an hour's rest and then he saddled up again. To rest any longer would help neither him nor the black. They needed desperately to find water down the trail, grass to keep them alive.

And what of Hope, the others on that circus wagon train? What would keep them alive? Ed was taking a desperate gamble. The thought nudged Shelter's mind . . . a desperate gamble. For what? To keep Blue from being angry, to keep from disappointing an audience?

Men don't gamble their lives out of such motives.

He had deliberately ignored Shelter's advice; perhaps Ed had deliberately left Shelter behind. There was no answer to these puzzling points, not here. But Shelter would have his answers.

The night was cold once more and the horse stumbled on through the maze of washes, rocky knolls and jumbled boulders. Shelter watched the stars, feeling his way south.

Sometime after midnight he felt the black could carry him no more and so he walked. He walked through deep sand and rocks, once painfully kicking a barrel cactus, imbedding a thorn in his toe. Then when Shelter could walk no longer, he crawled back into the saddle.

The morning exploded with light and heat and Shelter for the first time thought that he might not make it. He had the will, but the strength was rapidly waning. The black stumbled as it moved. It had eaten nothing for two days.

Distances began to mean nothing, and he found himself growing confused. The wagon tracks only appeared at intervals now, where the rocky surface gave way again, briefly, to sand.

He did not know the country well enough to be sure of where he was. Dry streambeds crossed his trail at intervals, lined with gray, dead cottonwoods. How far could the Nueces

River be? With a shock he realized that he might already have ridden over and through the Nueces. All of these southwestern rivers were seasonal to some extent, and the Nueces might have been merely another of those dry washes which lay behind him.

If that were true, then there would be no water until he hit the Rio Grande itself, and Shelter knew he would never make it.

He travelled on. The black plodded ahead, and mile after changeless mile slipped past, the only vegetation the crimson tipped ocotillo which towered over Shelter looking for all the world like giant squid poked head down into the sand.

It lay by the side of the trail and Shelter only glanced at it. A dead, now bloated lion, sand drifted into its mane. It was not another mile before he found a pair of horses, still in harness, and an overturned wagon shoved to the side of the narrow trail.

Death hovered over the desert, accepting all victims.

To the south those clouds still stretched from horizon to horizon, as they had since New Orleans. But overhead the sun was awesome. White through a brittle sky, it bled heat.

The land was empty, and Shell's eyes glazed with weariness. He saw nothing, and then he did, and it was enough to stand his hair on end.

They tracked across the trail, turned and

then paused. Thirty horses, all ridden, all un-shod. A party of Comanche warriors. They had found the circus train's tracks, paused to pow wow and then turned southward, riding the heels of Ed's wagon train.

Shelter kneed the black forward roughly, and the animal which had already given all it had, rolled its eyes back with a hurt expression.

But this was no time to worry about a horse, and Shell pushed it, riding hard throughout the long afternoon. It was late in the day, with the shadows creeping out from the can-yons, when he crested the low hill and sat in amazement, in disbelief, the lathered black quivering beneath him.

The river—it was the Rio Grande, and the shores of the shallow running river were lined with willows and cottonwood trees. The far side was Mexico, another country. It seemed incredible, but it was true.

Sunset colored the running river and quail called from the underbrush. Shelter led the black forward and they both drank deeply, Shell stopping the horse before it could drink enough to founder.

The bank of the Rio Grande was criss-crossed with tracks, and it didn't take an Apache scout to read them. The thirty warriors, those Shell had been following, had come to the river's edge, stepped down from their horses and waited a time—not long, it seemed. Then they had mounted and ridden away to the north. Why?

It didn't seem likely that the Comanche were leery of crossing into Mexico. These Indian warriors respected no borders.

It wasn't until he reached the Mexican side himself that Shelter was able to untangle the puzzle. The wagon train had crossed the river intact, and they had been met by a band of horsemen. A large band of perhaps fifty men. Together with this escort the circus had rolled southward.

"Now what do you make of that?" Shelter asked the horse. "Damned large contingent for the job. Whoever heard of a circus getting that kind of an escort?"

The horse did not answer, and Shelter could not puzzle it out, and so he withdrew into the trees where there was a bother of mosquitoes, and he rolled up to sleep, without eating. With the weariness he felt he was asleep in minutes, and he slept soundly until dawning.

The pueblo was small, of white washed adobe mostly, and there wasn't much of it. Tumbleweeds had piled up against the windward side of the buildings, two horses and a ragged burro were tied before the only cantina. The main road, if it could be called that, was rutted and pot holed. Planks, used to cross the muddy road during the last rain, lay imbedded in the hard clay.

All in all it was a dismal looking town, but to Shelter Morgan it looked like a bit of heaven. His food was gone, his horse weary, his shoulder stiff and painful. In his boot Shelter had four silver dollars, and he meant to see how many frijoles that could buy. He eased the black on down toward the sleepy pueblo.

The only two men on the street were asleep in chairs beside the weathered door to the cantina, but Shelter found the stable and a kid to rub his horse down.

Then he walked uptown, keeping close to the buildings where the only shade offered itself. There was a barber shop, the mustached barber asleep in his chair, and a big church set back from the street. They had a plaza where a fountain which wasn't working just then filled a blue tiled basin.

The peeling sign on the cantina advertised *comida*, and Shelter had seen no other place to eat and so he shouldered through the door, finding the saloon dark, musty, almost empty. He found a table in the corner and sat to it, putting his battered hat beside him on an empty, dusty chair.

"Senor?" The bartender was a big man with thin black hair and some broken teeth up front.

"*Cerveza, por favor. Tortillas y frijoles.*"

"*Bueno.*"

The man frowned and walked away, calling to the kitchen. "Conchita!"

She peered from the back room, a black eyed, brazen young woman wearing a black shirt and a red blouse which fell off her shoulders. She looked sharply at the barkeep and then at Shelter, her head tilted haughtily.

139

Shelter grinned in return and she tossed her head, going back into the kitchen. She was back in a minute, picking up a mug of beer from the counter as she passed. She set the glass down on his table, splashing a bit as she did so, then she placed down the steaming platter full of beans and fresh tortillas. Shelter had not ordered beef, but there was some *carne asada* thrown in and he dug in, drowning it in hot red chili sauce.

"All right?" the girl asked. She stood there, hands on hips, watching Shelter shovel down that food—the first he had tasted in two days.

"It's fine." He drank that beer in three thirsty gulps and wiped his mouth. "How about getting me *uno mas* before you get back to the kitchen, Conchita?"

Her eyes sparked but she picked up the mug, eyeing Shelter carefully. That blouse she wore fell down her olive colored shoulders and showed a deal of promising cleavage. Full, those breasts were, and smooth. Conchita tapped her toe impatiently.

"You see enough now?" she demanded.

"Not really," Shelter answered with a smile, and she spun away, going to the bar.

"Miguel, cerveza mas!"

She was a spitfire, all right, and she stared back challengingly at Shelter, but once he caught her looking at him before she had time to form that haughty little pout, and there was interest in her eyes.

Shelter ate the first half of that plate of

food quickly, but then he began to bog down. He sipped at the beer and watched the bartender, the two Indians who seemed the only living folks in this sleepy pueblo.

The saloon door opened just about then, and Shelter decided the town wasn't so sleepy as it looked. A big, black-bearded man wearing a huge sombrero and carrying a shotgun pushed on through the door and took up a position at the bar.

Behind Shelter another door opened and two men slipped in. Both of them were narrow of build, wearing mustaches, and both carried rifles in their hands.

Shelter began to feel uneasy. It wasn't so much the way these men were looking at him as the way they weren't. They purposely kept their eyes from Shell, but they kept on a comin', moving toward his table. Shell stretched and leaned back in his chair, letting his hand fall near his holster as he finished the stretch.

From the kitchen door he saw Conchita looking at him, and there was deep concern in those dark eyes. Shell fished two silver dollars from his pocket and put them on the table.

He would have to make his move, and he knew it. There were three of the Mexicans, all armed with long guns. They meant business.

He didn't wait to ask them what that business was.

There was a window behind Shelter and as

141

he casually scratched his neck he suddenly dove for it. A gun erupted as Shell hit glass and burst through the window, shards of glass flying everywhere. Bullets sang out, tearing at the window frame, the adobe walls and Shelter, in a crouch, ran up the narrow alley behind the cantina, lead whizzing through the air.

He startled a yellow dog which took off with a yipe, tail between its legs and ducked low as a shot ticked off the wall spattering plaster everywhere. Shell wriggled behind an empty rain barrel, saw a bearded face poke out of the window, and he fired, twice. The face withdrew in a hurry, a shout ringing out.

Shelter poked three fresh rounds into the Colt and looked around frantically. He was in big trouble, and he knew it. He needed to get to his horse and get out of town. Yet he did not even know how to reach the stable or if the alley he was crouched in led anywhere. If it did, he was damned sure they were there waiting.

His eyes went to the rooftops and making the decision quickly he clambered up on the barrel and stretched, but tall as he was he was not high enough to grasp the roof.

Cursing he jumped down. The alley was silent now, but he had no idea it would remain so. He looked around for something to place on top of that barrel, but there was nothing.

Then he saw her.

Conchita had appeared in a concealed side

door and now she waved her hand frantically. Shelter rushed to the door and watched as she slammed it behind him.

"Conchita . . . ?"

"Ssh!" She stood, ear pressed to the door, her hand lifted to silence Shell. Then he too heard them. Footsteps rushing up the alley and to the door where they paused and milled, low voices sifting through the door.

Shell could barely make out the voices, let alone understand the Spanish, but Conchita could and she listened intently.

"Get under the bed," she hissed and Shelter rolled under it. Conchita watched until he was concealed and then she flung open the door to the alley.

"What is happening? I heard shots!"

"Get inside," a voice growled. "The gringo tried to kill Ernesto."

"A gringo?" Conchita left the door to the room open and boldly walked outside, looking up and down the alley.

"I said get back in there, *estupida*!"

Conchita was shoved back into the room and the door was slammed shut behind her. She stood there smiling as Shelter peered out from under the bed.

"*Gracias,*" he said, standing, going to her.

"*De nada.* I jus' don' like to see a man shoot each other."

"Is that the only reason?"

She shrugged. "What do you think? You're so handsome I cannot bear it? All of you *hombres*!" She waved a disparaging hand and made a disgusted noise. But Shelter was grinning and her hard expression broke into a wide smile.

"You talk like you don't like the men," Shelter said, "I find it hard to believe. Looking at you . . ."

"What you are looking at is in your head," Conchita answered sharply.

"No, it's real. In the flesh," he replied, looking over those full, capable hips. "What is it, Conchita—did you have a bad experience, or was there never that special man?"

"*Si*, there was. A no good. *Se descarrio en su juventud.* He wanted to be a big bandito and shoot up people. But he was a coward, you know? And then he was nothing. *Bebía mucho, y pronto se arruinó.* He was, in the end only a drunkard with dreams of greatness."

"Drink has taken a lot of good men down," Shelter said quietly. The woman's face had grown meditative, now she threw the mood aside and asked, "but what can we do with you, *hombre*?"

"I've got an idea or two," Shell said slyly.

"Ah! You see!" Conchita said in frustration. "The man—one idea in his mind."

"And in a woman's if she'd admit it," Shelter responded.

"Maybe," Conchita agreed reluctantly. "Some —I don' know."

"No?"

"I said I don' know. I don' want to talk

144

about it. Tell me, why are you here? You only ride here to kill people, to make trouble for Conchita?"

"No," Shell laughed. "I got separated from my people. I'm with the circus."

"The circus?"

"Yes. Come on, Conchita. You must have seen a circus train pass through, with men escorting it."

"Yes," she said with reluctance, "I saw it."

"I need to catch up to it."

"Why?" Conchita faced him, her eyes sparking. "You are no circus man. I can see that."

"But I am," Shell said with a smile. "Temporarily, at least. I was scouting for them."

"A scout!" Conchita laughed mockingly. "A scout who loses his wagon train!"

"That's about what happened," Shelter had to admit.

"No. There is more involved," Conchita said incisively. "I know this."

"You think so?" Shell sat down on Conchita's bed and he took off his hat. "Why do you think so, Conchita?"

"Because I know La Condesa," she shrugged.

"La Condesa?" Shelter shook his head, not understanding.

"The countess—La Condesa Villa Real. It is to her rancho that the circus went. And La Condesa cares nothing for circuses, amusing things. La Condesa cares only for wealth and for power. Ernesto and the others—those men who came looking for you—they are La Condesa's men. And so I think that you are no longer with the circus, that the circus does not want you with it, that La Condesa wants you dead. . Therefore," she said quite solemnly, "you will soon be a dead man."

"I don't get this," Shelter told her. "I thought there was no more royalty in Mexico. But you've got a countess living here. You say she's a power-seeker; why bring the circus here all the way from Houston?"

"I could not say," Conchita said. "All I know is that La Condesa Villa Real is not a frivolous woman. It is true that Mexico is now a republic. But much goes on that is not republican. We are far from Mexico City, and we are a new wild land, senor. Like the Estados Unidos, I think."

"That's true. Much as Washington hates to admit it, there just isn't much government west of the Mississippi—none with any clout."

"Nor here. But La Condesa has this clout. And you, my friend are her enemy—for what reason, I do not know. But I know you will die if you do not leave Tortuga."

"That's something I just can't do, Conchita," Shell said, his blue eyes set. "There's business I have to attend to, and it looks for all the world like it'll have to be solved at the condesa's rancho."

"There is only one solution on that rancho, senor. All problems are solved by death. There is a big country back across the Rio Grande. Many places to be, to live. The condesa's ranch . . . that is a place men go only to die."

11.

It was dark and still Conchita had not returned to her room. Shelter stood in the deeply shadowed room, listening, watching, the faint scent of Conchita's powder filling his nostrils.

No one had come searching. Conchita had thrown them off the track with her boldness. Marching out there like that—had saved Shelter's bacon. It had also taken a deal of courage.

From beyond the walls Shelter could hear the sounds of men at their supper. Forks and knives clinked together in the dining room. Low voices mingled. Now and then there was a burst of laughter, and Shelter would have bet it was Conchita who triggered it.

She was quite a woman, that one. Bold, bright, and beautiful. Trustworthy? Shelter thought she was that too, but nevertheless he kept the door locked and his Colt near to hand.

He paced the floor, wanting to be moving, knowing he could not move far without help. They would be watching the stable, the road to La Casa Villa Real.

Still Shelter could make no sense out of this. Roland Blue, the circus, the Condesa Villa Real . . . there was a connection, but what was it?

Shell heard soft footsteps moving to the door and he pressed himself against the wall, Colt held beside his ear as a key turned in the lock and the door swung open.

Conchita entered and she was alone. In the darkness it was a time before she spotted Shelter. "You think I have come to shoot you?" she asked.

"Lately it's been hard to. tell who might start shooting," Shell said, "but no—I just didn't know it was you."

"Yes, it was . . ." Conchita hesitated and for a moment Shelter thought she would step toward him, but she turned away and became only a dark silhouette against the dimly lit window. "I have found a way for you to get to the Casa Real," Conchita announced without enthusiasm. "If you must get yourself killed . . . "

Shelter did not respond to that. He only watched her, wondering if she was thinking about that other man—the one who had wanted to become a gunfighter and get himself killed.

"Antonio Suarez is my cousin," Conchita said, turning suddenly back toward Shelter. "He will be taking a wagonload of hay to the rancho tonight. But first he will stop by here."

"All right."

"All right," Conchita repeated, nodding her head. "It is all right to die," she said with deep irony. "Of course. Then they will know you were a man."

"I can't explain it all now, Conchita," Shell answered, stepping nearer in the darkness, so near that he could feel the vibrance of her body, "but I am not doing this to win gold, to be heroic. It is a duty I owe to others. Men who have already been killed by the likes of the condesa."

"And so, if you die it will bring them back to life?"

Shelter did not answer. How could he? He didn't mean to spend his last moments with Conchita arguing anyway. He took her in his arms, but she did not respond. She was stiff, unyielding, but when Shelter pressed his lips to her throat, he could feel her pulse racing.

Slowly he kissed her lips, finding them

full, pliant. But Conchita did not kiss him back, nor did those full, sensuous lips part in response. She had been a long time without a man, this one, a long time in her grief.

"Antonio—he will be coming," Conchita said, and her words were shaky.

"When?" Shell kissed the lobe of her ear, her eyelids, "When will he be coming, Conchita?" he asked, his voice low, encouraging.

"Soon."

Conchita still did not answer Shelter's attentions, but she did not pull away either, and her eyes were closed in the darkness, her head thrown slightly back as Shelter's lips caressed her throat, as his index finger traced a rippling line across her shoulders and down to where her ripe breasts showed above the elastic of that red blouse she wore.

Shelter kissed her there and her hand lifted, just brushing his head. She made a small, empty protest, but again she did not pull away and when Shelter lifted his mouth again to hers he found her lips parted, moist and he kissed her hungrily.

Now slowly, Conchita came to life and when Shell cupped her breasts in his hands, kissing them again, she stroked his head, running her fingers through his hair.

He slipped the blouse down from her shoulders, allowing the breasts to come free. Ripe, full, warm beneath his lips. He took a nipple into his mouth and then the other, lavishing kisses on her flesh.

150

Conchita's hands were still on his head, and now one slipped to his shoulder, falling as if by its own volition to his abdomen and finally, with the least bit of hesitation to his crotch where she cupped the bulge in his jeans, her breath catching in her throat as she found it.

"Lie down," Shelter told her.

"Antonio . . . " she protested weakly.

"I'll lock the door," Shelter promised, and that seemed to mollify her. He crossed to the door and turned the key. Turning, he saw Conchita on her bed, the starlight through the narrow window glossing her naked body, her full, voluptuous hips, lighting her smile which was cautious, uncertain.

Shelter kicked off his boots and undressed. Then he crossed the room and stood naked before her for a moment, and he watched as she feasted her eyes on his lean frame, that great, erect cock. Then Conchita rolled onto her back, and she stretched out her slender arms to him.

Shell went down to her, feeling her thighs against his, her warm breasts against his chest. She kissed him then, gently at first and then more eagerly, and her hands went between their legs.

She wanted it her way, and Shelter let her have it. With one hand she spread and touched herself, with her other she searched Shelter's erection, his scrotum. Her eyes were distant, her smile mysterious, as she looked into his eyes.

151

She drew Shell to her and she positioned him so that she could stroke her clitoris with the head of his erection. Slowly she moved him against her, her fingertips also playing the game, her lips touching his with whispered kisses as she brought herself to eager heights.

Now she spread her legs slowly, letting Shell's cock enter her a bare fraction of an inch, the soft touch of her inner flesh, warm, pulsing, inflaming Shell's desire. He felt like slamming it home, filling her, but he held himself back, letting Conchita build to her apex of need.

They kissed again, deeply. Now she opened her pliant lips to his searching mouth, and her tongue brushed his lips. Her mouth was warm, soft, and it surrounded Shelter's like a delicate flower.

As they kissed her fingers inched him forward, drawing his shaft into her dewy, warm depths. She stopped suddenly and he felt her tighten inside. Conchita's hands went to his cock again and she rubbed it delightedly, then slipped momentarily between his legs to find and clutch his hard buttocks, to brush his balls.

Now Conchita drew him in again, and her heartbeat had begun to race.

"So much," she panted. "I never had so much."

Yet she wanted it all, wanted it badly and she pulled at him, her hips beginning to undulate. Conchita may have started slowly, but now she was building to a fever of desire.

She bit at Shell's chest as her hands went to his buttocks and dug at him. Her hips, strong, broad, eager, rolled and thrust at Shelter and when he touched bottom she cried out, throwing her arms around his neck, drawing his mouth to her taut, dark nipples.

The night was cool, but Conchita was on fire and she slammed her pelvis against Shelter, her fingers running everywhere, down his spine to his hips, between his legs where she could feel her own juices on him. Her mouth sucked at him and her breath was a panting in Shell's ear.

Now the juices gushed from her and Shelter could smell her rich, earthy scent. The blood was rising in him now and as he slid evenly in and out, her hands and lips inflaming him, Shelter could feel himself nearing a climax.

Yet he held back, letting Conchita ride the wave of her emotions to its turbulent crest. She shuddered and moved her hips against him almost desperately, her entire body thrashing wildly so that Shelter simply clung to her, letting her find her own points of pleasure, and still the juices, so long in coming, flowed from Conchita's body.

She trembled, hesitated, and then began to laugh. She laughed out loud as her body was filled by a raking, all-consuming orgasm which caused her thighs to quiver uncontrollably, her abdomen to cramp. Now Shell stiffened and swayed over her, working his cock in maddening circles, then driving it deeply inside as Conchita's breath caught with each stroke.

Shell felt his need building, and when he could hold back no longer he was joined at that peak of sensuality by Conchita who grabbed at his erection as he drove it home, her fingers milking him as he filled her with his hot climax.

She laughed out loud again as she reached a second, trembling climax, as Shell pulsed inside of her, slowly draining, and then her voice broke and she began to sob softly.

Shell petted her dark hair and kissed those soft shoulders and she responded with a hundred kisses, touching his arms, his shoulders, his neck as her hands ran up and down his thighs.

A last warm tear streaked her cheek, catching the starlight through the window and Shelter kissed that away. Exhausted, fulfilled, Conchita watched the tall man, a lingering smile playing on her lips as he continued to slowly move against her, letting the delicate glow Conchita still felt taper off instead of slamming shut.

"You, hombre. You are such a man . . . " She lifted her head and kissed his forehead. Then her arm slipped behind his neck. "I want to tell you . . . "

There was a knock at the door and whatever it was Conchita was about to say, Shell never heard. He rolled from the bed, snatching up his gun as Conchita, finding a blanket

154

to wrap around her, went to the door.

"Si?" She opened the door slightly and a shaft of yellow light painted the floor.

Shelter heard a few hurriedly muttered words and then the door closed again. Conchita turned and said, "Out the back door in five minutes. Antonio's wagon will be there."

"Well, that gives us five minutes," Shell said. He put his hand out to her, but she slapped it away.

"No minutes! Dress now quickly before they come to kill you."

She exchanged her blanket for a night dress which she wore as she peered out the curtained window. Shelter dressed quickly, strapping his Colt on as Conchita glanced at him.

She was pretty tough, all right. But the starlight showed the dampness in her dark eyes. Shelter pretended not to notice. Already she had unlocked the alley door, peering out to make sure the hay wagon was there.

"All right," Conchita said sharply. "Now go, no more fooling around, hombre."

"You're right," Shell said. "But I still figure I've got a minute," and he gathered the unprotesting Conchita into his arms, kissing her deeply, holding her near for a moment.

Then he was off, dashing toward the hay wagon where he slithered in as the voice of Conchita's cousin drifted from the cantina.

"No," Shelter heard Antonio say, "I just stopped for one beer. I have a delivery tonight."

Then Shelter heard a door close, felt the wagon rock under him as a big man clambered onto the seat. Then the wagon jerked forward and Shelter was rolling up the dark alley into the silent night.

He saw her only for a moment—a dark haired girl watching him from behind her curtain as the wagon travelled on, and then she was gone, gone into the loving night.

The wagon rolled on, up a long rutted road for mile after lonesome mile. Shelter stayed under the hay just in case. There was nothing else to be done, and so he watched the skies for a while, surprised to see that clouds were blotting out the stars. A wind rattled in the trees which lined the road here and Shelter smiled. It looked like they were going to get some rain. After all that time on the desert, *now* it would rain.

After an hour of travel Shelter felt the wagon slowing, he heard Antonio talking to the horses, heard the squeal of the brake. He wriggled back under the hay, holding his breath.

"*Que pasa, Antonio*?" someone said.

"Hay," Conchita's cousin answered. "For the animals."

"Hay? So late in the evening?" the man inquired suspiciously.

"*Si*, for the circus animals."

"I don' know nothing about that . . . " the voice grew louder as the guard circled the wagon. Shelter's hand tightened on the gun butt of his Colt. The hay caused his neck to itch and it scratched his eyes.

The man was resting against the wagon side now, by the shifting Shelter felt and he dug into the hay.

"*Caramba*, Miguel!" Antonio shouted in frustration. "It is only hay!" Conchita's cousin was sweating himself by now. His neck could be stretched as well if Shelter was found.

"What's the matter? You're so nervous?" Miguel asked. He was to the back of the wagon now and he ran a hand through the hay, passing within inches of Shell's face.

Now he could hear horses approaching and the guard pulled his hand back.

"What is it?" a third man demanded.

"Antonio Fuentes, with hay for the circus animals."

"Come on through. They've been waiting for you for an hour."

"*Gracias*," Antonio said with sarcasm. "And I have been waiting an hour to get past Miguel here."

"No one said nothing . . ." Miguel protested. By then the hay wagon was already in motion and the voices of the arguing guards faded into the night as Antonio guided the horses up a long, winding road.

At a switchback Shelter was able to look out and up at the great white hacienda which perched on the cliffs above. A beautiful, massive house of two stories with a red tile roof and great, shading oaks, it was lighted brilliantly just now. Some sort of celebration was going on—music drifted through the night.

Shell's face was set with grim determination. It had been a long trail, a bitter trail, but now he had his man, and he vowed, "Roland Blue, I hope you're enjoying that little party, because this is the last you'll live to see."

How he would do it, Shelter did not know. He was alone with only his Colt against an army of fifty hired guns, but he had sworn to take down Blue, and Shelter Morgan had never been a man to go back on an oath—Blue would die.

12.

The hay wagon made another bend and then stopped in the shade of some oaks. Shelter looked up quickly, seeing only Antonio.

"Get out here, *Señor, por favor.* Any closer to the hacienda and they may see you."

"*Bueno. Muchas gracias,* Antonio." Shell slipped to the earth and stuck out a hand which Antonio took.

"*De nada.* It was nothing at all, only, *Señor,* please never ask me any such thing again."

"I think this will be the last time," Shelter replied with a grin. It might be the last time he attempted anything, he reflected grimly.

"Good luck," Antonio said hastily, "*Via con Dios.* Now I must hurry along. If anyone is watching, they will wonder why I have taken so long."

Shelter slapped the man on the shoulder and watched as Antonio climbed back into the box, whipping his ponies forward up the steep trail. Then Shelter turned and climbed the bank behind him, slipping through the oaks which trembled in the wind.

The wind had built some and the rain which had begun with a few spattering, large drops, came in steadily now, screening the hacienda from Shell's vision.

Perhaps, he thought hopefully, that could work for him. It's not that easy to see a man on a dark, rainy night. Not if he uses his head. Besides, the guards would likely be trying to stay dry, sticking close to the buildings when perhaps they should have been out farther.

Shelter wound through the oaks. Below and to the south he heard a shout. Crouching, he listened, but it was only someone at the stables welcoming Antonio, hurrying him along.

Now Shell had a good view of the front of the hacienda, and he could see two men standing guard at the front door, a line of carriages parked around to the side. None of this made any sense, he supposed. Trying to break into this well-guarded house. But

160

it was that or wait for Blue to come out, and there was no telling when that might be.

No, Shelter's chances were really better now, with the darkness and the rain to veil him. Yet he needed some sort of an edge, and he was not likely to stumble over it at the front of the house.

He withdrew a way into the trees and began working his way toward the rear where entry might be easier. Then he froze. There was someone else in those oaks.

Pressed against the trunk of a massive, gnarled oak Shelter waited. Then he saw him. A man in a poncho and wide sombrero moving slowly through the trees. He moved sullenly, scuffing his boots, obviously unhappy with his duty on this evening.

He would grow even more unhappy.

Shell waited, careful not to move a muscle and as the guard slogged past Shell leaped out and without a wasted fraction of a second clubbed him behind the ear before the man could cry out.

Quickly Shelter stripped off the poncho and sombrero, putting them on. Then he tore up the guard's shirt, gagging him with it before dragging him to a narrow tree where he lifted the still groggy man's arms and strapped his hands to an overhanging limb using the guard's own belt.

The man's eyes were clearing now and he glared at Shelter, muttering a few choice words behind the gag.

"I know it ain't comfortable," Shell answered, "but it beats dyin', friend."

And there would be some of that on this cold night. Shelter pulled the sombrero down over his eyes and ambled through the oaks, scuffing his own boots once in a while now, trying to imitate the movements of the captured guard.

Suddenly he was out of the trees, and just beyond a patch of cleared ground lay a lighted window and a door—a kitchen by the smells which drifted through the rain. Shell glanced one way and then the other. Taking a deep breath he moved across the clearing, his hand locked onto that Colt beneath his poncho.

The rain was really coming down now, and the wind played at picking it up and launching it sideways through the night. Shelter was practically invisible until he reached the doorway where the circle of light painted him with liquid yellow.

He hesitated only a second before taking the doorknob and turning it, walking into the kitchen where a dozen men and women in white bustled about, preparing and serving food.

"*Que pasa, Chato*?" a woman hurrying past asked Shell.

"*Esta muy frio*," Shelter answered quickly, with, he hoped only a trace of accent. The woman stopped and glanced back, but Shelter broke into a coughing spell and she walked away, advising him over her shoulder.

"*Bebida cafe*."

Shell nodded, keeping his head down as his coughing continued, and when the woman was gone he moved toward the large coffeepot on the stove, but with a quick appraising glance he walked past it, choosing a door beside a huge pantry as a possibility.

It opened onto a narrow corridor and Shelter stepped quickly into it, his eyes darting to either end of it. There was no one there and he turned and strode toward the front of the house, hearing voices and laughter drifting in from somewhere.

Now he was in up to his neck, and he smiled faintly, thinking of what the Comanche had called him, and others before, "Crazy Shelter Morgan."

But there was no backing out and as long as Shelter had a load in the chamber of that Colt, he did not feel alone or helpless.

He rounded a corner in the corridor and pulled up short. Two armed men stood fifty feet away and they glanced up sharply at Shelter.

"Chato!" one of them called out.

Shell lifted his hand and turned away.

"Chato!" they called again, and now Shell's brain was pulsing with blood. He could hear their bootheels clicking on the tiled floor. They would round that corner in a second and when they did it would be obvious that he was an impostor.

Taking a chance he chose a door and, finding it open, he turned the knob and went inside, closing it softly behind him.

163

Then he turned, and when he did she was there.

"Hope!"

Her red hair had been stacked and pinned on top of her head and a strand of pearls was woven into it. She wore a green silk dress which brought out the outrageously deep green of her eyes. She glanced up with surprise from the vanity where she sat and then her lips formed an amused smile.

"Mister Jones! You actually did survive that desert."

"I did. But there's no time to talk about that right now. There's two gunhands in the hall looking for me. I need a place to hide."

Hope rose from the vanity, putting her hand mirror down. "Why certainly," she said, and that smile still played on her lips. "We can hide Mister Jones, can't we, Darling?"

Darling?

There was someone else in the room and now he stepped from behind a dressing screen, a chrome Smith & Wesson revolver in his meaty hand.

"Certainly," Roland Blue replied. "We can hide Mister Jones so well that no one will find him—ever again."

There was nothing Shelter could do as Hope slipped up beside him and lifted his Colt. He glanced at her with bitterness.

"How'd you ever get tied up with a bloody bastard like Sergeant Blue?"

"Simple," she shrugged. "I told you—I

needed money and he had it. He wanted the circus and I had that."

"Captain Morgan doesn't understand," Roland Blue said, his voice steely. "Captain Morgan doesn't understand money, that you have got to have it in this world or get kicked around like a damned stray dog."

"I guess I can understand a man feeling that way," Shelter said. "The part I couldn't understand, Blue was the idea that it was all right to butcher men to get that money you wanted so damned bad."

Blue moved in like a big cat and he back handed Shelter across the mouth, slamming his head back and filling his mouth with blood. Then, grinning, the big red-haired man drew back the hammer of that Smith & Wesson.

"So long, Captain."

"Roland! Wait." Hope caught his arm and then all their eyes went to the open doorway where the two Mexican guards stood watching.

"He broke in here," Blue said.

"He has Chato's clothes," one man said.

"We will take care of this man, Señor Blue."

"I can save you the trouble," Blue responded, his hand shaking with emotion as he levelled that pistol at Shelter. "No. No, señor, La Condesa would not like that. This is our job. Do not worry, he will be taken care of."

Each of the men took one of Shell's arms and he was rushed off down the hallway. A door was opened and then another, the music growing louder, the voices more audible.

165

Then he was shoved forward into a brightly lighted dining room. Faces turned up from the tables—Mexicans in dress suits, some wearing scarlet sashes sat dining in luxury.

And at the head of the table was La Condesa herself.

La Condesa. Shelter shook his head, wondering if Blue hadn't fogged his mind some with that blow. But as he looked again he was sure: it was the lady in white satin from the riverboat.

That same haughty expression, those same cool dark eyes. One of the guards, hat in hands, walked to the head of the table and he heard the woman erupt.

"What do I care! Do not interrupt me now, Santos. Lock the man up. I will see to it later." Bowing away the guard returned to where Shelter waited with the second man.

Shelter was dragged from the room, setting off a general murmur. He twisted his head back, staring at the woman, trying to evoke some sign of recognition, but there was none. And then the door slammed shut.

He was dragged back through the house which was a regular maze and thrown finally into a dark, low roofed room with a heavy oak door. One of the guards glanced through the iron grate set into the door and then they were gone, the lantern turned out, and Shelter was left alone in the darkness.

Just what in hell had he fallen into? Was La Condesa actually the woman from the riverboat or was it some remarkable coincidence? Shell's head rang and he could think only with difficulty.

He had to get out of that cell—that much he knew. If he did not then either Blue or La Condesa would take care of him for good.

He tried the door, but it was massive, hinged on the outside. There was a window, high on the wall, narrow, with iron bars set into the adobe. Shell went to it, peered out and tried the bars. Nothing. The bars were firmly fixed, and outside there was no help—only the driving rain, the lashing wind which pushed the cold water in through the window of his tiny cell, making the long, dark night even more miserable.

13.

Shelter's eyes flickered open in the night. The wind was howling like a banshee, slapping tree against tree, tearing the tiles from the roof of the hacienda.

He crossed to the window and squinted out, the wind hard in his face. A huge oak lay uprooted across the yard and the rain fell like silver buckshot. The road below was running water like a spring creek. The hurricane had finally made its way to shore, and it looked to be a bad one. The big, solidly built hacienda shuddered with each blast of wind.

Yet there were men out there, working. Wearing dark slickers, they struggled against the wind, their steps slow, leaden. There were twenty in all perhaps, forming a line from one of the circus wagons to an adobe outbuilding. Through the steel mesh of the rain, Shelter could barely make them out. The only light in all of the dark world was that produced by their wind buffeted lanterns. Yet he could see well enough to tell what they were doing.

The circus wagon's floor had been ripped up. It was the tiger's cage, and there was a dark, crumpled form in the front corner of the wagon which might have been the dead tiger.

They had torn up the planking of the floor and from beneath it now they removed long, shiny objects of some sort. Shelter wiped the rain from his eyes and strained to see . . . rifles!

It was rifles the wagons carried, that the circus had transported into Mexico, and now in the dead of this storm torn night they were being unloaded.

Shelter clung to the bars of his window a while longer, the cold rain on his hands and face. Then he slid to the floor and crossed to his rough bunk.

Rifles. So Blue was a weapons smuggler— it fit him better than the role of circus manager. That explained a lot, like why this circus had been moving so rapidly, with no heed to profit or schedule. And the Condesa—she was the buyer, obviously.

Those rifles explained quite a bit. Whatever their final destination, they were meant for some illegal purpose. Now Shelter knew with finality that he must die. He had stumbled onto someone's secret rebellion.

He stood, running a hand through his rain-dampened dark hair, and he went to the door, again trying to shake a bar loose, to find a weakness in that heavy planking, but there was none.

Shelter returned to the bunk, leaning back, hands behind his head. They had him—it was that simple. It would end as everyone had always predicted, as Shelter himself knew it must. They would simply execute him, and Blue and the others would ride free, wealthier than before, more smug.

He had obviously read Hope wrong, and he felt a vague regret about it. He truly had liked the woman, or the woman she had pretended to be. Well, it wasn't the first time he had been taken in by a female . . . although it was likely the last.

He found it hard to blame Hope entirely. After all, that circus was an uncertain venture. One shipment of guns could set her up for life. There are plenty of folks who will gamble on that one big chance out of desperation; maybe Hope was simply one of those.

The wind cracked like a whip and something on the roof, probably a chimney, caved in and clattered down the tile. It seemed like the world was blowing away out there.

Shell closed his eyes and then opened them again. He thought he had seen . . . and then he was sure. A dim light flickered outside of his door.

He slipped from his bed and went behind the door in the deep shadows, tearing a leg from the bunk for a club. They would doubtless take him down, but they would have a rough time of it, he vowed.

The light shone through the grate in the door, a thin, smoky light which barely reached the wall opposite and then a key turned in the lock and the door swung open.

Shelter hefted that club and nearly brought it down, but he saw the white mantilla, the dark hair and he held back. Whatever La Condesa was, he could not bring himself to do it.

She came into the dark cell, carrying a lantern. She was not alone. A tall man in a gray suit with a thin mustache, an American Shelter had seen somewhere—on the riverboat! Behind them was a third man, a Mexican of middle years with huge gray muttonchop whiskers, wearing a dark suit with a red sash and a fancy sombrero.

Outside the door there might have been another man, but Shelter could not be sure. They closed the door behind them and the lantern was placed on the floor, its feeble wash of light yellowing the packed earth floor. Shell stood facing them, that bed leg still in his big hand.

"You won't need that," the American man said.

"No?"

"Besides," he said with a quick smile, "it really wouldn't do you any good." He still held that pistol in his hand and Shelter nodded, lowering the club.

"All right, Mister . . . ?"

"My name is Tandy Luther," he answered. "And this is Señor . . . well, just call him Esteban."

"Can't say I'm exactly pleased to meet you," Shell answered. "I'm . . . "

"We are well aware of who you are, Mister Morgan," the woman interrupted. Her dark eyes sparkled even in that dim light, and she held her head regally, her back erect.

"You are?"

"Yes. We know about your business with Mister Blue, that you came here probably to kill him."

"Well now, you know all about me," Shelter said, his eyes fixed on the woman's face which was beautiful with those high cheekbones, those slightly full lips. "So why don't you tell me about yourself, before you kill me."

"We are trying very hard to keep you alive!" the woman flared up, "but you are making it most difficult, Mister Morgan."

"We were trying to keep you alive when we had you tossed off the steamboat," Tandy Luther put in.

"You were—it's an odd way of doing it.

172

I was damned near killed."

"You were in the way, sir," Luther said.

"In the way." Shell nodded. "Whose way?" he asked, lifting his eyes to Luther.

"In the way of your government, of the Mexican government."

"I think you'd better back up a little," Shell said, leaning against the wall, arms folded.

The wind shrieked outside and Shelter heard the branches of a tree being stripped off by the hurricane force. Tandy Luther had holstered his pistol, and now, with Esteban watching the door, he told his story to Shelter.

"We are government agents, Mister Morgan. Miss Elizabeth Townshend and I. The word leaked out that Roland Blue was smuggling guns across the border to supply La Condesa Villa Real and her separatist army. They wish, you see, to secede from Mexico, turning the entire state of Tamaulipas into a feudal kingdom — I can't imagine where people get these ideas," Luther said to the former Confederate before him, but Shelter did not smile in return.

"Why not let the Mexicans handle it?" Shelter wanted to know.

"Señor," Esteban said, "we are handling it, or trying to. But it is a matter which must be handled discreetly."

"We're far from Mexico City," Luther reminded Shell. "And La Condesa's forces are very strong. It would take an all out civil war to dislodge them."

"Yet you let Blue bring those guns across

173

the Rio Grande."

The woman interrupted impatiently, "We could hardly arrest him in the United States. There is no law, Mister Morgan, against carrying as many weapons as you like—until they are smuggled across an international border."

"We were afraid you would get to Blue before we did," Luther added. "That's why we had you tossed overboard from that steamboat. If Blue did not arrive with weapons, then none of these rebel chieftains would be assembled here. Our timing is very important."

"I don't get it," Shell insisted.

"You see, La Condesa is being held prisoner in Mexico City at this moment. Elizabeth, it was discovered after much searching, was a perfect stand-in. She is fluent in Spanish and bears a remarkable resemblance to La Condesa. Esteban is here quietly taking down the names of those who are attending our little gathering. One by one, without an outbreak of war, these rebels will be taken care of by the Mexican government."

"But none of them would be here if you had prevented Roland Blue from making his connection," Elizabeth said.

"All right. It's complicated for a simple man like me, but I think I got the picture. Now then—what are you going to do about Blue? And about me?"

"Blue will be arrested and charged if he returns to the United States . . . " Tandy Luther began.

"If!" Shelter exploded. "And if he doesn't? You can't mean you'd let him get away?"

"If we have to, to avoid blowing this entire operation, yes. He's not that important to us. Preventing a revolution is."

"He's important to me," Shelter said, his voice steely.

"This is exactly the reason we tried to discourage you from pursuing Blue, Morgan. You don't seem able to see the whole picture. When I wired Washington from Kansas City to obtain your background, they told me that you were a man obsessed."

"Obsessed. So that's what they call it these days."

"There's more at stake here than your revenge," Elizabeth said imploringly. "I know you are trying to repay people who had their lives taken from them by Roland Blue— but many other people, equally innocent, will die if we make a premature move to arrest Blue now."

"All right," Shell said, his temper cooling. "I guess I can understand that. What then? What about me? What do you want me to do?"

"We want you to go, before it's too late. When we leave, the door to this cell will be ajar. Make your escape now, under cover of this storm, Morgan. Forget Blue—it's the right thing to do."

"I guess it is the right thing," Shelter replied, his cool blue eyes searching their faces, "but I won't forget him. Not for a moment. Don't worry," he added for Elizabeth's sake, "I won't foul things up for you—you've got some guts yourselves, you two."

"If you'll take my hand," Tandy Luther said, stretching it out.

"I will—though I ought to break it for what you put me through on the river." Shell grinned despite himself and shook Luther's hand and Esteban's in turn. Elizabeth Townshend put out her hand as well, and Shelter took it into his rough, brown fingers, holding it for a moment longer than necessary.

Her eyes glittered with a meaning Shelter could not quite understand, and then, her head held high, moving with all the grace and elegance of a countess, she stepped through the door, following the two men. Then the lantern was put out, the cell falling to darkness.

Shelter waited a minute and then moved to the door. It was ajar, as they had promised, and he eased through, his eyes searching the darkness, not quite sure that it would be so easy.

Tandy Luther had left something behind for him. Sitting on the floor near the threshold was that Remington .44 he had been carrying. Shelter snatched it up and flipped open the gate, checking the rounds.

It was loaded. He now had a gun and to his right was a door leading out into the storm where an army could move right now without being seen. Yet he turned to his left.

"Morgan," he thought, "one day this contrariness is going to be the end of you."

But it galled him to think of Blue riding free. After the trail Shelter had ridden, to know that Roland Blue was in this very house — to turn and walk away from trouble was something Shelter had never learned.

He owed Blue, owed him plenty, and he meant to see that debt paid. Shelter opened the hall door a crack with the muzzle of his pistol and peered out.

It seemed deserted. Maybe every available man was unloading the rifles from the wagons before the storm got worse — if that was possible. There was a crash behind Shelter and he spun around. The wind had blown a window from the frame and it lay on the floor, broken into a thousand pieces, the branch of a tree protruding through the empty frame.

Shell moved out into the corridor. The floor plan of the house was a maze, designed purposely to confuse intruders, it seemed, but Shelter felt certain he knew the way to Blue's apartment.

He heard footsteps approaching and he again stepped into a side door. This time he was lucky, the room was unoccupied. He took a look through the keyhole, but he could see nothing but shadows moving past. By the sound it was two men in boots.

Shelter gave them a minute to get around the next bend in the hallway and then he stepped out, moving swiftly through the darkened house. Dark it was, but far from silent. The wind seemed to take hold of the house and shake it, twisting it on its foundation. And the Hacienda Villa Real was a massive structure, solid as rock. Shell wondered fleetingly how Tortuga itself was faring.

The little town lay square in the middle of a dry streambed. Even up this high Shelter had seen the rain pouring off the already sodden hillsides, building a short-lived, but tumultuous river.

Shelter made a bend in the corridor and then he heard voices. Pressing himself to the wall, he listened, but he could make nothing out. He thought the third door was Blue's room. Was that where the voices came from?

If Blue was not alone . . . Shelter shook it off. He had come too far to worry about that. He took ten long strides and then he was there, his hand resting on the bronze door handle.

Shelter paused and he thumbed back the big hammer of that Remington. He had begun to twist the door handle when the voices came again and he froze.

It was Blue who spoke. And the voice which answered — it was Elizabeth Townshend. The voices were just behind the door now and as Shelter took a rapid step backward, the door swung open and Elizabeth came into the hallway, followed by Hope and Roland Blue.

14.

Roland Blue stepped out into that hallway, his gun digging into Elizabeth's back. Hope was right behind them, and through the open door Shelter saw the body of Tandy Luther lying in a pool of blood.

"I always thought there was something fishy about you, Countess. When those *banditos* find out who you are . . . "

It was Hope who first saw Shelter, and her mouth opened in a silent scream. Blue's eyes flashed that way but it was too late. Shelter had taken one step forward and now he chopped down with his gun, slamming the barrel down against Blue's wrist.

Blue's gun clattered to the floor and Shelter took him by the throat, shoving him up hard against the wall.

Elizabeth, reacting quickly, had picked up Blue's revolver and she held it on the two of them, though a mite shakily.

"It's time to pay the piper, Blue," Shelter said. His voice was soft, but those eyes were hard, his jaw set.

"Thank God you're here," Hope said. She took Shelter's shirt sleeve but he shook her off.

"You can't walk both sides of the street, Hope." He glanced at Elizabeth.

"What happened?"

"They must have suspected somehow. They overheard Tandy and me talking." Her eyes opened wider. "Tandy!"

"Don't look. He's dead," Shelter told her. He had Roland Blue by the throat still, and the big man's eyes were bugged out of his head. If he just kept tightening that grip . . .

"Morgan." Elizabeth's voice shook his thoughts clear. "We've got to get out of this house."

"Out there?" Blue sputtered in disbelief. The hurricane still raged; they could hear its roaring through the walls.

"It's a good place. Nobody would hear a shot."

180

"That damned rain . . . !"

"You won't have to worry about it long," Shelter said coldly.

"You wouldn't," Blue said, but there was no conviction in his words. "You wouldn't shoot me down cold, Morgan."

Shelter glanced at Elizabeth who was watching him worriedly and back to Blue who was red in the face, shaking. "No, damnit! I wouldn't. Let's take us a ride."

"We don't have a chance," Elizabeth said.

"We damn sure don't have one here. Let's move it."

Shelter let go of Blue, shoving him ahead so roughly that he almost fell. Hope followed, her face drawn to a mask.

"We can make a deal, Morgan," Blue said across his shoulder.

"I don't understand money, remember."

"I can't go back . . . I don't want to hang," Hope said over and over.

"Don't worry," Shelter told her. "They don't hang gun runners. Unless . . ." it came to him suddenly. "Where's Ed?"

"He . . ." Hope's eyes went pleadingly to Blue who only shrugged sullenly.

"I didn't think he was in on this," Shelter muttered. "Poor Ed. He was only stupid. He only stuck with that rag tag circus on your account, I expect." Hope started to say something but Shell silenced her. "Don't say anything. You'd only make it worse."

They had reached the door and Shell motioned

with his pistol for Blue to try it. The door was swollen in its frame and he had to give it a good yank. And when it did come open, with all that wind behind it, it slammed open, driving Blue against the wall, nearly tearing itself from the hinges.

The hallway was filled instantly with hard rain and howling wind. Blue cringed next to the floor.

"Go on!" Shelter yelled. "Get moving or by God, I *will* shoot."

It was worse than Shelter had thought. Outside the wind and rain were the only presence. The limbs were torn from the oaks, cracking like cannon fire. A circus wagon rolled across the yard, bouncing into the air before a ferocious gust.

There was no one moving out there. A man would have to be crazy to try it. Shelter went ahead, Elizabeth clinging to him. Blue was knocked from his feet and driven against the wall of the hacienda. He cowered there, his face bloodied, his nose broken and for a moment it seemed that not even the threat of Shelter's gun could induce him to rise again.

But rise he did and they staggered on through the rain torn night. Shelter wanted to make the stables if that was possible. They could never make a getaway on foot. Of course . . . maybe there was no way anyone could escape, not in the middle of this storm.

As if to accentuate this thought a young tree whipped past Shell's head, thrown as if it were a matchstick. There was a narrow ditch Shelter had noticed which wound around toward the stables, and he hoped to slip down it, out of sight.

"Morgan!" Elizabeth shouted. They had come to the ditch. The only trouble was it was now a roaring freshet. White water gushed down the chute, tearing at the banks. Glancing back, Shelter could see that the water rushing off of the hills behind the house was undercutting the hacienda itself.

"What now? Elizabeth shouted again. She added something else but her voice was lost in the wind.

"We've got to get horses! Horses!" Shell answered, pointing toward the stables.

Elizabeth shook her head. There was something else on her mind.

"The gunshed!" Elizabeth shouted, cupping her hands. "Tandy was going to blow it up. There's a charge set!"

Shelter turned that way and then looked back toward the stables. They had to be going, and now, but blowing that shed where the rifles were stored would almost certainly defeat this revolution before it got started.

"All right! I'll give it a try." Shelter crouched down with the others behind a giant oak. The limbs of the tree waved frantically like a thousand flags. The gunshed was just beyond the clearing. Shelter knew it would be tough to start a fuse in this weather, but he would try it. He knew one other thing—if there was a guard anywhere who hadn't been driven under cover by the hurricane, he would be watching that shed.

"Keep your gun on him!" Shelter told Elizabeth.

Hope sat wide-eyed beside the tree, her hair in a tangle, her face empty of expression. She kept looking helplessly to Shelter Morgan, and he felt a pity for her. Her plan, so carefully worked out, had come down around her ears. Her world was blowing away.

As Shelter stood she stood with him. "Morgan!" Hope cried out. "Wait for me!"

"Sit down!" he hollered. "Just sit there!"

Then, with a glance at Elizabeth, he was gone, running into the wind, the footing treacherous under his boots. The ground was sodden, the rain an iron screen across the earth.

He had come again to the ditch which frothed with water moving at a locomotive's strength. He would have to leap it, and though it was only five feet the banks were caving in, and were liable to do the same under his weight.

Beyond, the adobe shed stood, a part of its roof blown away. Shelter took a few steps back and then made his dash, jumping as far as he could. Even then it was barely enough. The wind was full against him, and it slapped him back hard. Landing, Shelter felt the bank give beneath him. His legs went in up to the knees and suction held them in as he tried to pull them out. He clawed at the bank and finally wormed his way up and over, but when he straightened and glanced back he saw something that scared the living hell out of him.

"Hope! Go back!"

She was standing there like some mad Fury, her red hair wild in the wind, her dress pressed against her body as she lifted a white hand to Shelter through the storm.

"I'm frightened. I don't want to be with Roland anymore. Let me stay with you!" Hope screamed. Water trickled across her face and the wind tore at the fabric of her dress.

"Get back!" Shelter yelled. "Just get back. That bank . . . !"

But it was already too late. The raging water tore away at the bank under Hope's feet and Shelter saw her go. She slid forward, grabbed desperately for a handhold and found none. The wind covered her shriek as she tumbled into the roaring freshet, the white water boiling over her, sweeping her away.

Shell had a last glimpse of her white face, those wide emerald eyes, and then she was gone, torn away by the night and the storm.

He stood there a moment, the wind buffeting him, the water rushing away, and then he turned, moving in a crouch across the clearing, slipping through the storm to the rear of the gun shed.

The fuse was there, where Elizabeth had described it. He cleared away the mud and debris and, glancing around, he tried to start that fuse in the only way available.

He shoved the muzzle of that Remington down next to the fuse end and fired. The fuse flared up, sparkled and then fizzled out.

He fired again, the shot no more than a loud clap against the tumultuous roar of the hurricane, and the fuse caught fire again, dancing away, sparking as it ran.

Shelter got to his feet and as he did he saw a rain-soaked dark face peering around the corner of the shed. He fired twice and the face disappeared. Then he turned and ran, ran for all he was worth. Elizabeth had not said how much explosives were planted there, and it could be plenty.

The footing was bad, the wind driving, and twice Shelter went down. He zig-zagged as he moved toward the woods, not even knowing if someone was shooting at him through the storm.

He leaped the ditch again, noting that the water was nearly overflowing now, and hit the woods just as the charge in the gun shed caught and the day, dark as it was, was splashed with brilliant white light, streamers of fire curling against the dark background as the explosion, nearly silent, caused the earth to tremor.

That would finish it with those weapons. They all would not be damaged, but they would be blown from hell to Hades, covered with mud before this was over. Those that were recovered—the undamaged ones—would have to be disassembled to the bare parts, cleaned, oiled and reassembled before they would be any good.

The storm had kept the guards inside the hacienda, huddled together for protection; the explosion brought them out of the woodwork like swarming insects. Shelter saw them moving across the yard, carrying lanterns and guns, pointing and motioning wildly.

He darted through the woods, his heart racing, his breath ragged. He clambered up the small knoll to where he had left Elizabeth and Roland Blue—she was gone!

Shelter looked around desperately. He was sure this was the place . . . could he have been mistaken?

A bit of white cloth lay near the tree. White satin. This had been the place, but somehow Blue had overwhelmed Elizabeth. Perhaps when Hope had distracted her. Maybe Hope's dash was no wild-eyed notion, but a calculated distraction—a calculation which had gone wrong.

Behind Shelter dozens of men raced to cover the stables, fanning out across the clearing. The rain seemed to be lessening, the wind stilling, and Shelter felt a chill of apprehension.

If that storm broke . . . they were coming, and there were plenty of them. He had no horse and too few rounds of ammunition. And somewhere behind him was a man who wanted to see Shelter Morgan die more than he wanted anything on God's earth. And now Roland Blue had a gun too.

The important thing just now was that Blue had Elizabeth Townshend. Blue would be banking that Shell was coming after him—and he was right.

With that Remington dangling in his hand, Shelter moved through the wavering shadows, his flesh cold beneath the rain-soaked clothing he wore. The wind made it difficult to keep his balance as he dipped into a hollow and made the trees on the far side.

Despite the darkness and the screening rain, Shelter was able to follow Blue's trail. The footprints cut deep into the mud, and the girl was dragging her feet, making a slow go of it for Blue.

Yet he would not run far, Shell knew. He would pick his spot and lie in wait, gunning down Shelter from ambush—if Shelter allowed it.

The wind shivered the oaks. The rain was lighter now, but it stung exposed flesh like bee stings. The shadows moved frantically, making vision untrustworthy.

They stepped suddenly into Shelter's path and his gun snapped up. But Shelter never pulled the trigger.

Roland Blue stood there, his puffy face broken by a mocking smile. He had a pistol trained on Shell, and he had Elizabeth in front of him for a shield, his arm crooked around her throat to hold her.

"Hello, Captain," Blue said triumphantly. He managed a dry, cackling laugh. His hair hung across his face in dirty strands and his hooded eyes glared with hatred. "It's a long way from Georgia. There's been nights I lay awake worrying about you—wishing we would have killed you back there. Especially after I heard some of the things you been up to."

"Like what?" Shell asked, trying to buy some time. There was no way he could shoot and be sure he would not hit Elizabeth. Blue's arm tightened around the woman's throat, choking the breath off as Shelter took a tentative half-step forward.

"Like what? You killed General Custis, I heard. Colonel Fainer."

"That's right. They had it coming. Same as you, Blue. Same as you."

"Only this time it's going to be different! This time you're going down, you son of a bitch!"

He was ready to kill. Shelter could see it in his eyes. The cords on Blue's throat went taut and he flinched as if to make his move.

Elizabeth moved first. She stood strangling in front of Blue, but Shelter had never seen a woman as cool as this one, and she was cool now.

Her hands were bunched into fists and as Shell saw Blue twitch, Elizabeth felt it. She moved her hips slightly to the side and then with all of the strength she could muster she slammed her fist back into Blue's groin.

Blue's gun exploded into the air and he lost his grip on Elizabeth. Shelter saw the girl slip down and he fired through the rain at Blue, seeing a splotch of red appear on Blue's collarbone.

Blue fired again, missing wildly as Shelter ducked behind a tree. Shelter fired off-handedly from behind the rain darkened trunk of the oak and then rolled out, coming to his feet, his gun ready, but Blue was gone.

Blue was gone, but Elizabeth was there, unhurt, sitting on her bustle in the mud, her legs flung out, her hair hanging in damp ringlets across her shoulders.

Shell moved forward cautiously, eyes searching the night.

"He's gone," Elizabeth confirmed. "Took off like a rabbit. He's a man who wants to live. That bullet of yours scared him. He didn't have what it takes to stand up to you on even terms."

"That's just what he'll have to do," Shell said, shoving the pistol behind his belt, "sooner or later."

He stuck out a hand and Elizabeth took it. He pulled her to her feet. "That was quick thinking, what you did."

"They gave me a crash course on self-defense. I hated every minute of it. Now," she smiled, that same smile Shelter remembered from the steamboat, "I'm glad I spent that time learning a few things—although it seemed a waste of time."

"It's never a waste of time to spend a few hours learning how to take care of yourself.

For a man, and especially for a woman, it can save a tragedy. There's a world full of Roland Blues out there, believe me."

Shelter looked into her dark eyes and grinned, "Besides, taking those lessons enabled you to save my bacon. And I'd like to think I'm worth something."

"I'm starting to think you are, Mister Morgan. Just who you are, what you are, how *much* you're worth, I'm not sure yet. But I'm starting to think you are worth something, too."

With a start Shelter realized that it had nearly stopped raining. The wind was heavy in the trees, but it was gusting to perhaps forty miles an hour, not double that as it had been in the middle of the night.

Looking to the south Shelter was shocked to see a deep crimson line drawn along the horizon as sunrise pierced the gray mass of clouds.

"It's letting up," Shelter said.

"It's not over. It's the eye of the hurricane. It will be calm for a time, and then the storm will hit again just as hard as before," Elizabeth told him. Shelter turned his eyes to hers.

"If it's clear for only an hour, that's too much for us. They'll have all the time they need to find us and hang a rope around our necks."

Elizabeth stood there silently, stunned now as she realized that what Shelter had said was true. They had tricked a gang of bandit kings. Taken their money, destroyed their goods. There would be no mercy shown.

Now she could see them sifting through the oak woods, searching. And still the skies cleared. They had nothing to fight back with. Only the two handguns, one of them half-empty.

That and the determination Elizabeth read in the tall man's blue-gray eyes.

It would have to be enough.

15.

The skies paled to an eerie yellowish orange,
though circled around them were massed,
thundering clouds for as far as the eye could
see. Below the hunters moved through the
woods and Shelter turned, taking Elizabeth's
hand as they made their way deeper into the
oaks.

He did not mean to stand and fight, nor
did he think it was possible. What Shelter
wanted was to buy time. An hour, maybe

longer—how much longer he did not know. He wanted time for the hurricane to set in again, to again cover the world with a wash of rain and wind, giving them a chance of escape.

The trouble was that the grove of oaks was just that—a grove, and not a deep forest where a man could lose himself. The searchers would be bound to come upon them sooner or later.

There was no way to plan against that; it would have to be left to chance. Perhaps they would find a hiding place, or a way to slip into the foothills above them. To the north, east and south the land was flat desert. Glancing toward Tortuga, Shelter was shocked to see nothing at all remaining of the sleepy pueblo.

A new river, hundreds of yards wide, moved toward the sea. Even the Casa Villa Real had been undercut, seemed to be sagging toward one face. It had not been built to withstand such weather—nothing is.

Shelter climbed higher, leading Elizabeth who was having a rough go of it. Finally as they sat together, panting for breath, watching the relentless pursuit below, he told her, "It's that dress, Elizabeth. You're carrying extra weight, and your legs are all bound up by it."

She didn't even hesitate. Standing she slipped off the long satin gown and with Shelter helping, she hollowed out a hiding place in the ground where they threw the dress, covering it again with leaves.

"There," she panted, "now I'll be able to run a little better." Untying her corset she shoved it under the leaf litter as well, "And breathe a little better."

"Besides all that, you look a whole lot better," Shelter said. He searched her body which was full, appealing, clothed now in only a petticoat and undergarments. Her breasts strained at the fabric of her chemise and Shell smiled with appreciation.

"At a time like this . . . you certainly do have a one track mind."

"That's the way Nature set me up, Elizabeth. I can't go against my nature, can I? Why, that wouldn't hardly be right. Beauty turns my head, and that don't seem wrong to me. And you're as beautiful just now, with your hair all frazzled and your face streaked with dirt, as anyone I ever saw."

Elizabeth made a small, vaguely disapproving frown, but when Shelter turned his head, he saw her smile from the corner of his eye.

He sat drawing deep gulps of the cool air into his lungs. Just below he could see two men in leather jackets winding along the creek bottom, and one of them lifted his eyes to the knoll where Elizabeth and Shelter sat.

Shelter sat unmoving, and for a moment he thought the man had not seen them. Suddenly his hand went up, however and he let out a shrill whistle which curled the hair on Shell's head.

"They've spotted us," he told Elizabeth. "Let's get moving."

He yanked her to her feet and they withdrew into the woods as a lone, searching shot whined off the trunk of a tree.

"All right," Elizabeth panted. "Where now?"

That was a good question. One Shelter had no answer for. Above and behind them the foothills rose to the sky, but they were washed with rain in the arroyos, denuded on the rocky slopes above.

It was a nasty climb with no good cover. They could be picked off like sitting ducks.

There was no good choice; the only way to handle it seemed to be to wind through the trees, moving silently, changing direction constantly—hoping for help from the skies.

But the hurricane seemed to hang dead in the skies as it had for days before it finally hit; and though there was terrible weather— winds, hail and rain—all around them for hundreds of miles, it was a balmy, bright morning here.

Shell took Elizabeth's hand and they clambered up a steep slope which was studded with jagged boulders. It was rough going, but they needed the rough terrain between them and the pursuers.

They clawed to a narrow shelf, their fingers raw with the climbing, their legs cramped, and as Shelter straightened up to reach the next level a dozen shots ricocheted off the rock face, spattering them with rock splinters. Shell smothered a curse, ducked low, and they crawled along the shelf, bullets whining off the rocks around them.

They made the trees again, and—Shell thought and hoped—the pursuers could not be sure they had made them. He hoped they would believe them still to be on the rocky shelf, and bullets still slammed against the hillside stone.

Shell and Elizabeth wriggled into the woods and lay gasping for breath in the cool shade of a massive oak, Shelter's arm around Elizabeth as they watched the backtrail.

Far across the canyon he saw a man in the open, and his finger tensed on his trigger. Yet he did not want to fire, knowing that would be a giveaway.

The man slipped through the shadows, and then he was gone.

It echoed across the canyon suddenly, tightening Shell's stomach, causing his muscles to go taut.

A terrible, violent scream shot through with anguished despair filled their ears. It rose again, a wavering, sickening scream and then it was suddenly cut off.

A man had died, and horribly.

"What was that?" Elizabeth asked, but Shelter had no answer. They slipped deeper into the woods, moving in a half-circle around the perimeter of the oak grove, their pursuers more numerous now, nearer.

Somehow they had gotten up behind Shelter and Elizabeth. Pausing for breath they could hear them moving down from the direction of the foothills, closing the circle. Below

Shelter was a small, steeply sloped sink which was clotted with willow and vine hung oaks. They moved that way now, taking to the deeper cover where they would have a chance of eluding their enemies until the storms came again. The air was heavy, still, no breath of wind ruffled the leaves as they slid into the teacup sized valley, the brambles and branches tearing at their flesh.

"Shelter, we . . . " Elizabeth began to speak but Shelter took her roughly to the ground. He pointed up and now she could see the men ringing the valley. They lay utterly still in the high brush, the minutes passing into hours. They had not chosen this hiding place, but it would have to do now.

There were twenty men up on the rim, and if they didn't know that Shelter and Elizabeth were trapped below, they seemed to have a good idea that it was so. They worked their way down the long slopes, criss-crossing through the brush. It was only a matter of time.

There was no hope of waiting until dark — darkness was hours away. The only hope they had to cling to was the hurricane. If the hunters saw it coming that alone might be enough to send them scurrying back to the hacienda.

Looking up Shelter saw nothing but clear skies traced across by thin wisps which could hardly be called clouds. That hurricane was a slow, plodding thing giving no heed to the wishes of the small men it surrounded.

"Back," Shelter whispered. He motioned

with his head. He thought they could wriggle back into the deeper brush where a man might walk right past them without seeing them, and so they tried, moving backwards inch by inch, over rough stone and through heavy manzanita brush.

It was slow, painful work. As they inched back, Shell tried to smooth the marks they made in the damp, dark earth with his hands, scattering leaf litter over the tracks.

A good tracker could run along the trail they were leaving; but maybe they had no good trackers among them. Hope piled upon feeble hope as these thoughts ran through Shelter's mind, twisting, colliding, finally withering as they found no substance to sustain them. They were only the straws a desperate man clutches at: maybe they would be safe in the deeper brush, maybe the hurricane would chase them off, maybe the bandit chiefs were not skilled trackers.

"Look," Elizabeth whispered, touching his shoulder.

Shell rolled over, looking behind him, surprised to see that the land fell away dramatically there. A deep, quite narrow gorge cut by water, where water still ran, twisted invisibly through the heart of the chaparral thicket.

"Go on down," Shell breathed into Elizabeth's ear. "But watch that water."

Cautiously she slipped into the gorge which was all of thirty feet deep, but only a few feet wide. It was a fissure carved out of solid rock by some tool of nature—water or earthquake—but there were outcroppings a man could step on, and work on down out of the thicket toward the desert beyond where with luck no one would yet be searching.

Shelter could see a pair of boots through the brush as he followed Elizabeth, slipping over the edge and into the fissure. Cautiously they moved down stream, the white water gushing around their feet as they picked their way from rock to rock. Elizabeth suddenly slipped and Shelter's hand shot out, gripping her wrist tightly as he held her back from the raging waters.

She turned and nodded her appreciation, a wan smile flickering across her lips. Then again they moved forward, the stream roaring past underfoot, filling the air with spray.

It was slow, arduous work, yet each tentative step forward along the gray, water-washed rock took them a little farther away from the pursuit, from death.

It seemed the bandits did not know of this chute. If they did, then somebody would be posted below where the fissure petered out as the water ran out onto the desert floor. That was a sobering thought; but it was a risk they had to take anyway. There was no other choice.

It was another gruelling half an hour before Shelter could see that the gorge was gradually becoming shallow, although around the sharp, final bend in the cut he could not yet see the outlet.

And then they were around the bend, and Shelter could see the desert. There was a small stand of wind broken sycamores, some sage and nopal cactus and then the yellow desert which for all its emptiness looked like a chunk of the Promised Land to his weary eyes.

Finally they were out of it, clambering up the slick side of the chute to level ground. The foothills seemed far distant. The hacienda itself was invisible. Shell lowered himself to the damp earth, sitting beside Elizabeth who nudged his shoulder.

"Look," she said, "here it comes again."

Looking out across the desert he could see a wall of gray from horizon to horizon. The sand blew before the winds. The hurricane was coming in again, and hard.

"Just in time to cause us more trouble. Let's get moving, Elizabeth. We'll need a place to sit this out."

She took a deep breath, her breasts rising and falling behind the damp material of her chemise, and reluctantly stuck out a hand. Shelter helped her to her feet and they moved off through the sycamores, Shelter's head turning back constantly to make sure there were no bandits following, and he saw none.

The hurricane which had seemed incapable of movement that morning now roared across the desert flats at locomotive speed, tearing at the earth as the winds growled a warning.

The trees already bent before its weight as if in surrender.

"If we can ride this out, we'll have made it," Shelter said. A voice behind him responded.

"I wouldn't be so sure of that, señor."

Slowly Shelter turned and as he did he came face to face with a mustached bandito. The man had a toothy grin on his face and a Winchester in his hands.

"You have a lot of heart, señor, but you cannot beat the odds, eh?"

"Not this time, it seems," Shelter answered.

His gun was holstered and that bandit's rifle was cocked, ready to fire. The man had him and he knew it.

Again the wind rumbled and slapped against Shell's clothing, tugging at his sleeve. The bandit was still grinning but then he glanced up and the grin fell from his face, washed away by the panic which followed.

Shell frowned, and then he heard it. A low growl which was not of the storm, and he turned his head just slightly. There it was, in the tree.

"My, God!" Elizabeth gasped. She gripped Shelter's arm tightly.

"Hold still," Shelter said. "Just stay still, Liz."

She did. She stood utterly frozen, her eyes wide as she stared into the low limb of the sycamore. The big cat glared back with yellow eyes, its every muscle tense beneath a glistening black coat.

Set free by the hurricane, the black leopard was prowling, and it was mad.

"That's what happened back in the hills," Elizabeth said with a shudder. "That scream we heard. That man dying—it was the leopard."

"Him or another one," Shell agreed. "That brush might be crawling with them. The hurricane tore their cages to pieces." Her hand tightened on his arm again, and Shelter ordered her, "Just stay still, Elizabeth. Don't move a hair. It'll be all right."

But the bandit was not remaining still. His eyes were wide, shifting from Shelter to the crouching big cat and back. Slowly he backed away, his rifle still on Shelter, and then he stumbled over a rock.

Shelter heard the cat hiss, saw the bandit leap to his feet, and in panic take to his heels. Then a black, silky shadow flashed past his head as the leopard made his dash.

The bandito made a good thirty feet but then the big cat hit him, taking the man down by the haunches. Then the leopard was all over him, mauling, tearing at his throat.

Elizabeth buried her face against Shelter's shoulder. Shell pushed her gently aside and then he took a chance and stepped out, recovering the bandito's rifle. The cat turned its head and snarled. Its muzzle was stained with gore now, and Shelter knew that the cat, having learned to take down a man and kill him, would likely remain a man eater. Still the bandit twitched, and Shelter would have killed the leopard, but he knew the shots would bring others on the run. It was the bandit's life or that of Elizabeth and his own. He only backed away, watching as the leopard picked the man up by the neck, and straddling him, dragged him into the deeper brush.

"They should have fed them," Shelter said.

The winds were stiffening by the moment and now the first, huge drops of rain hit them. Shelter glanced at the thundering skies and took Elizabeth's arm.

"Let's find us a place to hole up. Looks like we'll need it."

They moved toward the desert; and the rains built. The wind hit them with the shock of a triphammer suddenly, driving them both to the ground. Rising, they struggled on through the thinning chapparal, the clumps of cactus and stone, searching for a place, finding none.

Once they saw a male lion slinking through the brush, and later a monkey, still wearing a red cap, peering in confusion from a stand of mesquite.

The rain was blotting out the world once more, the wind tearing at the shivering brush, and movement of any kind was difficult, let alone effective movement. Shelter held tightly to Elizabeth's hand, fighting against the wind, moving into its teeth, searching for a cubbyhole of any kind, something to cut the bite of the wind, the sting of the rain which was now so heavy that Shelter could barely make out Elizabeth through it.

They stumbled on, their clothing sodden, the wind ferocious, their course a blind one.

And then he saw it.

They were nearly past it before Shell managed to pick it out of the all-obscuring grayness. He tapped Elizabeth's shoulder and jabbed a finger toward it.

"Up there!"

She could see nothing, but she moved that way. There was a low rock face ahead, dotted with clumps of nopal and sumac, and behind one such clump Shelter had caught a glimpse of a dark shadow where none belonged. Coming nearer he saw that he had guessed right.

A low, indistinct smudge against the rocks which ran heavily with water now, the cave was only three feet high at the mouth. Shelter flung a rock into it, and it echoed hollowly. There might be snakes or even—now—a tiger in there, but they had no time to make these decisions.

"I'll go first!" Shelter hollered above the storm, and he wriggled through the gap in the rocks. The roof of the cave was low, and water seeped through the red stone, but Shelter called back. "Come in, Liz!"

It wasn't much, but it was better than being outside. Discounting the discomfort, the danger of being hit by flying debris, the chance that they might stumble into another bandit's guns, there was a constant, very real danger of a severe flash flood out on that flat. The cave, raw and damp as it was, was a haven for the time being.

The wind quieted as Shelter crawled ahead

into the cave, and surprisingly it opened up until the roof was nearly five feet high. Then the tunnel dead-ended in a chamber some twenty feet wide. The walls were smoked with the soot of ancient fires. In that soot some ancient hand had scratched a stick figure of a man and a representation of an elk. An elk—how long ago had that been when elk roamed this desert? Ages ago, many camp-fires ago.

The cave had been used more recently too, but not often. Elizabeth sat shivering as Shelter scraped up the remains of a pack rat's nest and used the small twigs in it to start a small fire. The smoke must have a way to escape—others had used this cave to dry themselves in. And he had no worry about the smoke being seen outside against the gray mass of the hurricane.

"It's like a bit of heaven," Elizabeth said. "To be dry—out of danger. Why, I can hardly hear the wind."

The fire had caught and now it crackled pleasantly. The red stone of the cave walls reflected the warmth.

Outside it was storming, but here it was cozy, warm, with room to sit comfortably. It felt fine. Now Shell's eyes lifted to those of Elizabeth. Her eyes were firebright, her face calm, beautiful. Steam rose off her clothing.

Shelter grinned. 'It wouldn't be a bad idea to slip out of those wet things."

"You haven't," Elizabeth said. Her eyes met

206

his, wandered across his lanky frame, studying those broad shoulders, the leathery toughness which was Shelter Morgan.

"I didn't want to disturb you any," he answered.

"And my undressing . . . ? That wouldn't disturb you?" Elizabeth asked, her lips now blossoming into a full, sensuous smile.

"Lady," Shelter replied. "I'm so damned disturbed right now, just looking at you, that I don't think even that could make it any worse."

"No? Let's see about that."

Elizabeth stood and kicked off her petticoat. That left only her chemise which she slipped off her shoulders, revealing soft white flesh. Her eyes were haughty, amused, as she watched Shell's eyes react to her. She drew it down and her breasts came free of the fabric. Like ripe peaches, they burst forth into the firelight, full, smooth succulent. Shelter's eyes were riveted to their soft contours, the pink nipples which embellished their smoothness with focal points of sensuality.

Slowly she slipped out of her chemise, wiggling it down over her hips which were broad, smooth, perfectly contoured. Then she stood naked before him, the firelight painting her body. Shell's eyes searched her inch by inch, settling on the luxuriant dark bush between her thighs where a narrow ribbon of pink showed.

"Well?" she demanded.

"I was wrong—you managed to get me plenty more disturbed."

"It's your turn," Elizabeth said challengingly.

Shelter could not stand in the low cave and so he simply kicked his boots off and unbuttoned his shirt. Elizabeth's eyes glittered, watching as each button came undone, liking the broad chest of Shelter Morgan, the dark hair which grew there.

Then he slipped out of his jeans and as his huge erection came free Elizabeth licked her lips and moved to him, lying down next to the dully glowing fire on the bed Shelter had made of his clothes.

She kissed him and there was a fire in her kiss that sent a tingle of electricity up Shelter's spine and caused his cock to quiver.

"It's not much of a bed," Shelter said, drawing her down to him, his hands cupping those magnificent breasts, his eyes meeting those dark, sparkling eyes of Elizabeth.

"We don't need much of a bed." She kissed his mouth, turning her head slightly, her lips soft, steamy. "This is a perfect place. Warm, hidden. Out there . . . " her eyes changed expression, briefly, revealing a little girl beneath that composed womanly exterior, "I was so frightened. I moved in a daze."

"You did fine." Shelter's fingers ran up along her shoulder, stroking that fine dark hair which glowed with the firelight.

"I was scared out of my wits. If it hadn't been for you . . ." Her lips grazed his chest.

"If it hadn't been for *you*, you mean," Shelter corrected. "Blue was going to kill me, remember? That was a cute trick you pulled on him."

"I also do it with the open hand," Elizabeth revealed and Shelter lay back, smiling as Elizabeth's hand slid to his erection, gently manipulating it, her thumb tracing patterns across the inflamed head of it, running down the shaft with just the tenderest pressure. She cupped his balls in her warm hand and kissed his lips deeply, her breasts pressed against his chest.

"How's that?" she asked.

"You know any other tricks?" Shelter asked with a smile. He put his hand behind her neck and drew her head to him, kissing that ripe mouth through the screen of glossy, dark hair as Elizabeth slipped on top of him. He felt her hand deftly shift his cock and then he was inside of her, sinking into the warmth, the sweet depths of the woman.

She fell against him, her cheek beside his, her hair over both of them like a soft coverlet. Slowly she moved against him, and she spoke to Shelter in a low, quavering voice.

"It's so big. My, you have a nice one . . . mm. Nice and . . . oh, God! That was a good spot. Right there. I want to take it all inside of me. I want to . . . " her hand reached back, finding Shell. "I want to stuff your balls inside of me."

She twisted her head and her mouth, moist and warm, found Shell's. She kissed him, letting her tongue linger inside of his mouth as her hips rose and fell, as she smeared herself against Shell.

Shelter's hand reached down between them, running across her tense abdomen to her thighs and she spread her legs eagerly, wanting his touch as she wanted his shaft buried in her.

"Yes . . . can you find it? Right there," she breathed and Shell's fingers stroked her soft inner flesh, found the rigid tab of pink flesh there and Elizabeth quivered under his touch. "That's good. That's very good," she repeated childlike as she swayed against him and then she groaned. The sound came from deep in her throat and Shelter felt her go tense, felt the gush of fluid against his fingers, felt the demanding pressure against his cock, and she kissed him again, destroying his ability to hold back with her pliant mouth, the shuddering of her hips, the sweet, soft moaning.

He began to arch his back, to drive into her while his fingers still toyed with the soft, quivering flesh between her legs.

"Yes," she whispered. "Yes. Do it again, higher. Harder." Elizabeth clung to him, encouraging him, her body slick against his, her flesh warm. "Harder. Slam it home. Harder . . . " Her voice broke off into an expression of delight. "Mm! Again. Mm!"

Her teeth teased his ear lobe and she whispered, frantically, "All the way in. All the way to your balls. Yes. God, yes, Shelter. Now fill me. Please. Fill me with it."

Her body writhed crazily now and her hips drove against him, her head turning side to side, her teeth nipping at his flesh and Shelter felt himself reach the point of no return.

Arching his back he drove it home and drove it again, holding his position for a long minute as he did come, filling her with his warm fluids and she breathed softly. "Thank you, thank you. Yes."

She kissed his neck, his chest as Shelter's erection throbbed spasmodically, as her inner muscles milked him dry, as his hands clenched her full, firm hips, holding her to him.

The fire died down and it went to darkness, but the cave was warm, Elizabeth was warm against him. Shelter felt the tension drain out of him, the anger and hatred. Outside somewhere it was storming; outside somewhere Roland Blue lurked wanting to kill. But just now none of it mattered and he clung to Elizabeth, feeling her lingering kisses still his racing pulse, her body warm against his in the night.

16.

Shelter's eyes flickered open in the darkness, and for the moment he was lost in forgetfulness. He tried to claw the sleep from his eyes, his mind. Where . . . why? And then he was aware of the warm, feminine body next to his own, shifting in her sleep, and the memories came back in a rush.

What had awakened him? He frowned against the darkness, and then it came again—an odd, whistling sound. The storm?

The storm. A sudden wave of guilt washed over Shelter. He had been sleeping and soundly. Now was not the time for that. In order to survive he and Elizabeth must be moving as soon as the hurricane waned, as soon as travel was possible. He shook Elizabeth and her eyes opened.

"You'd better get dressed."

"Already?" She smiled dreamily. "I'd just as soon stay here."

"So would I. But if we stay here a few more hours we're liable to have to live out our lives in this cave. We've got to move, Liz. Rise and shine." He kissed her and then slapped her bare ass smartly.

He found enough tinder left to build a tiny hatful of fire and they dressed by that.

"Still wet," Elizabeth complained.

"No matter—they wouldn't have stayed dry long. Once we get outside . . . "

That odd, squeaking noise interrupted Shelter and he looked quizzically toward the mouth of the cave. The noise, strange as it was, was somehow familiar, but he couldn't put his finger on it.

"What *was* that?" Elizabeth asked worriedly. Shelter could only shake his head.

"I don't know."

"Shelter?" Elizabeth asked softly. Her head was turned away slightly as she buttoned her chemise. "If we do get away from here . . . what then?"

"Then? Then I find Roland Blue."

"You've got to be kidding!"

"No," Shell said seriously. "Not at all. Why do you say that?"

"You'd start again? Another episode like this one?"

"It's what I set out to do," Shelter said, but the puzzlement lingered on Elizabeth's face. The fire dwindled, flickered and then was snuffed out.

"Come on," Shelter said. He got to hands and knees, and not forgetting that sound he carried the rifle ready as he crawled toward the mouth of the cave.

Now the sound of the shrieking wind came to them strongly, and there was water on the floor twelve feet inside the crawlway. It was still storming out there, and it was bad.

Reaching the entrance to the cavern Shelter froze, awestruck. The entire canyon was awash with water. The rain swept down out of the foothills, fanning out onto the desert floor. It was deep, and it was moving fast.

Elizabeth was at his shoulder. "How are we going to get across that?" she asked in a hushed voice.

"We aren't," Shell answered, "unless . . ." It came again, that strange, mournful sound and through the sweep of the rain Shelter saw it standing there, head bowed.

"Nancy!"

"There's a *woman* out there!" Elizabeth asked incredulously, but Shelter, grinning, shook his head. And then Elizabeth saw it too, standing miserably in the bitter storm—an elephant.

"Her name's Nancy," Shell said. "A casual acquaintance of mine."

"You meet them all eventually, don't you?" Elizabeth laughed. More seriously she added, "The poor creature. She needs to be in a barn somewhere."

"No," Shelter disagreed. "She needs to be right where she is. Nancy's our ticket out of here."

"You're joking!"

"Not at all. It would take a hell of a horse to cross that floodplain . . . assuming we had a horse. But Nancy could make it. Look at those legs. And the important thing is," Shelter pointed out, "we've *got* her."

"She's so huge!"

"But gentle. I think she'd take some comfort from a human hand just now. Like I say, I've met her. And I've seen how she's ridden."

"Yes," Elizabeth said dubiously. "But can *you* handle her?"

"I'm going to have to, I guess. We need that animal, Liz. Need her bad. We not only have to get across that river to get away . . . it's possible they'll come after us if they can pick up our trail. We'd never have a chance afoot.

"Look at those legs," Shelter said, eyeing the elephant, "I'll wager she can run a bit."

"How do you ride it?" Elizabeth asked. "To sit astride that back, you'd have to spread your legs . . . " she blushed and Shelter grinned.

"You can handle it." He drew her to him and kissed her, feeling a tingle from those lips. His hand slid down and patted that wonderful rear end.

Then he slipped out into the blasting winds, and through the rain he worked toward where Nancy, her great head hanging mournfully, watched his approach.

He talked gently to her, not wanting to frighten her, and Shelter thought he saw some response in her eyes. They say an elephant doesn't forget, and maybe she did recall Shelter and the handouts he had given her.

"Hello, girl," Shelter said. He patted her shoulder and Nancy's trunk flickered toward him, resting briefly on his shoulder. "Bad weather for men and elephants, isn't it?" He patted the elephant's shoulder again, then walked around her, assuring himself the great creature was not injured. She appeared sound.

The next step was recalling what he could about the way Tramp Garber had handled Nancy.

He went to her head again and took that enormously strong trunk in his hand. Strong, it was, but Shelter knew it could also be incredibly gentle. It had been with Tramp Garber at least.

Uncertainly he took a deep breath, and he turned around, moving closer to the elephant.

"Up, Nancy," he said. There was a hesitation, a seeming reluctance. This man was not her trainer. But then she wrapped that trunk around Shell's waist and raised him high into the air.

When she had him over her massive head she gently unwound the trunk from him and Shelter was able to scoot onto her back. Then, as he had seen Garber do, he took her ear. He slapped it twice, only pats to Nancy, and she began to move, slowly plodding away.

In the wrong direction. Shelter tugged on that ear and she came around, like a well-trained horse. And why not? She was well-trained, and as smart as a cow pony. She had to be to perform her stunts.

With a little experimenting Shelter was able to guide Nancy back toward the cave mouth where Elizabeth stood in the rain, waiting.

Stopping her was something else, but after several tries Shelter got the hang of that too.

"I thought you were pulling out on me," Elizabeth said, looking up at the mounted man.

"Not hardly. It just takes some getting used to."

Shelter leaned down and gave his hand to Elizabeth, pulling her up behind him. The wind was a howling demon, the rain a wash of cold drops of steel, but Nancy was firm as rock beneath them, and Shelter turned her northward, across the floodplain and toward the desert beyond as the wind screamed a protest. Elizabeth hung on tightly, her arms around

217

his waist, her face buried against Shell's back as the cutting wind twisted her black hair into mad confusion, as the ambling behemoth beneath them waded the frothing river.

There was no way a horse could make that crossing, and Shelter felt a little better. He was still worried about pursuit, but now he was certain they could not be followed—not until that pounding rain stopped anyway.

Nor were they leaving a trail anyone would be likely to follow. An elephant's tracks would be a curiosity to the trackers and little more.

They plodded on through the heart of the hurricane, the wind buffeting them, the water washing over them in torrents. Yet with Nancy under them they felt secure. She must have been uncomfortable, but she plodded on as if none of it bothered her.

Shell simply held tightly to the elephant's ear and Elizabeth clung to him, her eyes closed, her hands now and then taking teasing excursions.

On the afternoon of the second day the skies began to clear once again, the rain to fall off, and sunset was a brilliant crimson and gold display through the far off storm clouds.

The water which had run off the hillsides in torrents now stood only in ponds, the desert having swallowed up the hurricane's floods almost overnight.

They found a meadow where gramma grass and some buffalo grass grew thickly, and together Shelter and Elizabeth pulled enough to feed Nancy. Her appetite was voracious, but the grass came up easily from the saturated earth.

Wearily they lay against the grass, watching as Nancy fed, as the clear, sundown sky faded to a clear, warm night with clusters of diamond like stars lighting the surprised heavens.

"It's ended," Elizabeth said, snuggling up to Shelter's shoulder. "I can't believe it. The hurricane has blown away. No one is following us. All ended." She kissed Shelter's shoulder and smiled.

"Not yet."

"You mean Roland Blue?"

"That's right—he's running free out there somewhere. I mean to find him."

"And do what?" Elizabeth asked.

"Take him in. Now there's charges against him. Gun-running, murder."

"Yes." Elizabeth nodded, remembering Tandy Luther who had been a tough, dedicated man.

"He'll hang," Shelter said, "and I'll be there to see it." He was silent then, watching the stars. Then he felt Elizabeth's tug at his arm and he turned slowly to her, falling into her kiss.

Morning was clear and warm. The sun, so long absent, was pleasant on their backs. Nancy walked ahead easily, more content herself now with the end of bad weather and a belly full of grass.

They came down out of a dry, rock arroyo

and onto the cactus studded flats. Beyond lay the desert, clean, yellow in the brilliant sunlight. The Rio Grande cut a wide, blue-gray swath across the sands.

"Now we are safe," Elizabeth said. "No matter how badly they want us, those bandit chiefs won't cross into the States to find us."

She was right and Shelter's spirits lifted a little. Elizabeth squeezed him tightly and kissed his bare back. As they came onto the flats a dry breeze rose to meet them, and Elizabeth's sunbright hair drifted across Shelter's shoulders. Nancy slogged on patiently beneath them.

And then they were there, all around them with the sun glinting on the weapons they held in their hands.

Comanches. Hungry-looking, dangerous men with a hatred for anyone not of their tribe, with rifles primed for killing. They leaped in front of Shelter, and Nancy stopped. Then the Comanches crowded around.

Awestruck, they circled the incredible animal which had inexplicably appeared on their desert. This grand horse ridden by a brazen white who traversed their land with only his rifle and his nearly naked squaw.

In their eyes Shelter read a variety of feelings. Some appeared to take this animal as a sort of omen, others were simply curious, and in a few faces Shelter read the lust to kill.

Their leader, a man of forty or so, with a badly scarred chest and a broken nose stepped forward, arms crossed. He studied Nancy and then Shelter for a long minute before lifting his finger accusingly.

"Who are you, devil? What sort of pony is this you ride from out of the wind?"

"I am your friend," Shelter said quietly. His eyes were cool, but his hand on the Winchester was sweaty, tense.

"What sort of friend! Demon, ghost, warrior?"

"I will tell you, Iron Heart!" a voice interrupted. Shelter looked around to see a young man approaching. He wore badges of rank knotted into his hair, and he wore a bear claw necklace. He also moved with a limp, and Shelter recognized him as the young brave whose leg he had set away back at the watering hole.

"You know this white, Tall Pony?"

"I know him." The brave smiled and looked up at Shell. "He is Shelter Morgan. Crazy Shelter Morgan. A white man, a crazy white man who makes friends of the Comanche enemy, who rides great horses from out of the wind. He is my friend, Iron Heart."

"No white is our friend," another, sour-looking brave shouted angrily.

"He is," Tall Pony replied, his voice brittle.

"No. He must die," the tall brave answered. He was looking at Elizabeth in a way that revealed just why this Comanche wanted Shelter out of the way. "It is the law, Iron Heart. Your law!"

Iron Heart nodded slowly, looking from one brave to the other, then he decided.

"This is a crazy man, this Shelter Morgan. A spirit has taken him for its own, made him crazy. Given him a strange devil horse to ride. No good will come of killing a spirit man. Go, Shelter Morgan!" Iron Heart commanded. "Go before you are killed. Before your heart is given to the sands, as it was with him."

Iron Heart pointed to the inert figure which lay near a clump of nopal cactus. It was a man, dead. His chest had been carved open, his eyes put out, his scalp taken.

It was Roland Blue. Paper money lay scattered across the ground all around him.

"I will go." Shelter nodded coolly, though his throat was dry, his muscles knotted. Slowly the ranks of Comanches moved back and he nudged Nancy forward, lifting a hand to Tall Pony. The young brave nodded but did not smile or lift an answering hand.

With their eyes upon them Shelter urged Nancy forward, down the long slopes toward the Rio Grande beyond. Elizabeth finally dared a look back, and when she did, the Comanches had disappeared. Gone, to a man. The sands seemed to have swallowed them up, and she sighed with relief, leaning her head against Shelter's back, holding him still tighter as the elephant, smelling the fresh water, moved with eagerness toward the Rio Grande, toward Texas.

Suddenly Elizabeth laughed, a joyous, deep

laugh. Shelter glanced back at her as the elephant lumbered toward the river. "What is it?"
he wanted to know.

"What is it?" she laughed again, at length
until she had to wipe the tears from her eyes.
"This was my first job with the government."

"Yes," Shell encouraged her.

"I'll have to return to Washington . . . Shelter," she gasped for breath as another wave of
laughter overcame her. "Do you have any idea
how *this* is going to look written down in my
report."

Shelter grinned, thinking of the bureaucrat
who would frown and scratch his head over
the elephant. He shook his head, taking in a
deep cool breath of the desert air.

"It's liable to cause some muttering," Shell
agreed.

"Disbelief!" Elizabeth corrected.

"Maybe."

"Maybe you ought to leave it out," Shelter
suggested.

"Maybe so," Elizabeth said thoughtfully.

"And don't forget—this mission isn't over
yet. Not until you're back in Washington."

"It's all over but the shouting," Elizabeth
answered, kissing Shelter's bare, sun-warmed
back.

"That's just it—it's time we got to the shouting . . . that is, if you'll leave that part out
of your report, too."

"And if I don't?"

"If you don't," Shelter grinned, "then I'll

promise you you'll have the liveliest report any agent ever turned in."

He turned then and he kissed her, holding her close to him as Nancy waded across the sun-glossed Rio Grande, Texas stretching out before them.